BASIL THOMSON
RICHARDSON SCORES AGAIN

SIR BASIL HOME THOMSON (1861-1939) was educated at Eton and New College Oxford. After spending a year farming in Iowa, he married in 1889 and worked for the Foreign Service. This included a stint working alongside the Prime Minister of Tonga (according to some accounts, he *was* the Prime Minister of Tonga) in the 1890s followed by a return to the Civil Service and a period as Governor of Dartmoor Prison. He was Assistant Commissioner to the Metropolitan Police from 1913 to 1919, after which he moved into Intelligence. He was knighted in 1919 and received other honours from Europe and Japan, but his public career came to an end when he was arrested for committing an act of indecency in Hyde Park in 1925 – an incident much debated and disputed.

His eight crime novels featuring series character Inspector Richardson were written in the 1930's and received great praise from Dorothy L. Sayers among others. He also wrote biographical and criminological works.

Also by Basil Thomson

BASIL THOMSON

RICHARDSON SCORES AGAIN

With an introduction by
Martin Edwards

DEAN STREET PRESS

Published by Dean Street Press 2016

All Rights Reserved

First published in 1934 by Eldon Press

Cover by DSP

Introduction © Martin Edwards 2016

ISBN 978 1 911095 69 9

www.deanstreetpress.co.uk

Introduction

SIR BASIL THOMSON's stranger-than-fiction life was packed so full of incident that one can understand why his work as a crime novelist has been rather overlooked. This was a man whose CV included spells as a colonial administrator, prison governor, intelligence officer, and Assistant Commissioner at Scotland Yard. Among much else, he worked alongside the Prime Minister of Tonga (according to some accounts, he *was* the Prime Minister of Tonga), interrogated Mata Hari and Roger Casement (although not at the same time), and was sensationally convicted of an offence of indecency committed in Hyde Park. More than three-quarters of a century after his death, he deserves to be recognised for the contribution he made to developing the police procedural, a form of detective fiction that has enjoyed lasting popularity.

Basil Home Thomson was born in 1861 – the following year his father became Archbishop of York – and was educated at Eton before going up to New College. He left Oxford after a couple of terms, apparently as a result of suffering depression, and joined the Colonial Service. Assigned to Fiji, he became a stipendiary magistrate before moving to Tonga. Returning to England in 1893, he published *South Sea Yarns*, which is among the 22 books written by him which are listed in Allen J. Hubin's comprehensive bibliography of crime fiction (although in some cases, the criminous content was limited).

Thomson was called to the Bar, but opted to become deputy governor of Liverpool Prison; he later served as governor of such prisons as Dartmoor and Wormwood Scrubs, and acted as secretary to the Prison Commission. In 1913, he became head of C.I.D., which acted as the enforcement arm of British military intelligence after war broke out. When the Dutch exotic dancer and alleged spy Mata Hari arrived in England in 1916, she was arrested and interviewed at length by Thomson at Scotland

Yard; she was released, only to be shot the following year by a French firing squad. He gave an account of the interrogation in *Queer People* (1922).

Thomson was knighted, and given the additional responsibility of acting as Director of Intelligence at the Home Office, but in 1921, he was controversially ousted, prompting a heated debate in Parliament: according to *The Times*, "for a few minutes there was pandemonium". The government argued that Thomson was at odds with the Commissioner of the Metropolitan Police, Sir William Horwood (whose own career ended with an ignominious departure fromoffice seven years later), but it seems likely be that covert political machinations lay behind his removal. With many aspects of Thomson's complex life, it is hard to disentangle fiction from fact.

Undaunted, Thomson resumed his writing career, and in 1925, he published *Mr Pepper Investigates*, a collection of humorous short mysteries, the most renowned of which is "The Vanishing of Mrs Fraser". In the same year, he was arrested in Hyde Park for "committing an act in violation of public decency" with a young woman who gave her name as Thelma de Lava. Thomson protested his innocence, but in vain: his trial took place amid a blaze of publicity, and he was fined five pounds. Despite the fact that Thelma de Lava had pleaded guilty (her fine was reportedly paid by a photographer), Thomson launched an appeal, claiming that he was the victim of a conspiracy, but the court would have none of it. Was he framed, or the victim of entrapment? If so, was the reason connected with his past work in intelligence or crime solving? The answers remain uncertain, but Thomson's equivocal responses to the police after being apprehended damaged his credibility.

Public humiliation of this kind would have broken a less formidable man, but Thomson, by now in his mid-sixties, proved astonishingly resilient. A couple of years after his trial, he was

appointed to reorganise the Siamese police force, and he continued to produce novels. These included *The Kidnapper* (1933),
which Dorothy L. Sayers described in a review for the *Sunday
Times* as "not so much a detective story as a sprightly fantasia
upon a detective theme." She approved the fact that Thomson
wrote "good English very amusingly", and noted that "some of
his characters have real charm." Mr Pepper returned in *The
Kidnapper*, but in the same year, Thomson introduced his most
important character, a Scottish policeman called Richardson.

Thomson took advantage of his inside knowledge to portray
a young detective climbing through the ranks at Scotland Yard.
And Richardson's rise is amazingly rapid: thanks to the fastest
fast-tracking imaginable, he starts out as a police constable, and
has become Chief Constable by the time of his seventh appearance – in a book published only four years after the first. We
learn little about Richardson's background beyond the fact that
he comes of Scottish farming stock, but he is likeable as well as
highly efficient, and his sixth case introduces him to his future
wife. His inquiries take him – and other colleagues – not only to
different parts of England but also across the Channel on more
than one occasion: in *The Case of the Dead Diplomat*, all the
action takes place in France. There is a zest about the stories,
especially when compared with some of the crime novels being
produced at around the same time, which is striking, especially
given that all of them were written by a man in his seventies.

From the start of the series, Thomson takes care to show the
team work necessitated by a criminal investigation. Richardson
is a key connecting figure, but the importance of his colleagues'
efforts is never minimised in order to highlight his brilliance.
In *The Case of the Dead Diplomat*, for instance, it is the trusty
Sergeant Cooper who makes good use of his linguistic skills and
flair for impersonation to trap the villains of the piece. Inspector
Vincent takes centre stage in *The Milliner's Hat Mystery*, with
Richardson confined to the background. He is more prominent

in *A Murder is Arranged*, but it is Inspector Dallas who does most of the leg-work.

Such a focus on police team-working is very familiar to present day crime fiction fans, but it was something fresh in the Thirties. Yet Thomson was not the first man with personal experience of police life to write crime fiction: Frank Froest, a legendary detective, made a considerable splash with his first novel, *The Grell Mystery*, published in 1913. Froest, though, was a career cop, schooled in "the university of life" without the benefit of higher education, who sought literary input from a journalist, George Dilnot, whereas Basil Thomson was a fluent and experienced writer whose light, brisk style is ideally suited to detective fiction, with its emphasis on entertainment. Like so many other detective novelists, his interest in "true crime" is occasionally apparent in his fiction, but although *Who Killed Stella Pomeroy?* opens with a murder scenario faintly reminiscent of the legendary Wallace case of 1930, the storyline soon veers off in a quite different direction.

Even before Richardson arrived on the scene, two accomplished detective novelists had created successful police series. Freeman Wills Crofts devised elaborate crimes (often involving ingenious alibis) for Inspector French to solve, and his books highlight the patience and meticulous work of the skilled police investigator. Henry Wade wrote increasingly ambitious novels, often featuring the Oxford-educated Inspector Poole, and exploring the tensions between police colleagues as well as their shared values. Thomson's mysteries are less convoluted than Crofts', and less sophisticated than Wade's, but they make pleasant reading. This is, at least in part, thanks to little touches of detail that are unquestionably authentic – such as senior officers' dread of newspaper criticism, as in *The Dartmoor Enigma*. No other crime writer, after all, has ever had such wide-ranging personal experience of prison management, intelligence work, the hierarchies of Scotland Yard, let alone a desperate personal fight, under the unforgiving glare of the media spotlight, to prove his innocence of a criminal charge sure to stain, if not destroy, his reputation.

Ingenuity was the hallmark of many of the finest detective novels written during "the Golden Age of murder" between the wars, and intricacy of plotting – at least judged by the standards of Agatha Christie, Anthony Berkeley, and John Dickson Carr – was not Thomson's true speciality. That said, *The Milliner's Hat Mystery* is remarkable for having inspired Ian Fleming, while he was working in intelligence during the Second World War, after Thomson's death. In a memo to Rear Admiral John Godfrey, Fleming said: "The following suggestion is used in a book by Basil Thomson: a corpse dressed as an airman, with despatches in his pockets, could be dropped on the coast, supposedly from a parachute that has failed. I understand there is no difficulty in obtaining corpses at the Naval Hospital, but, of course, it would have to be a fresh one." This clever idea became the basis for "Operation Mincemeat", a plan to conceal the invasion of Italy from North Africa.

A further intriguing connection between Thomson and Fleming is that Thomson inscribed copies of at least two of the Richardson books to Kathleen Pettigrew, who was personal assistant to the Director of MI6, Stewart Menzies. She is widely regarded as the woman on whom Fleming based Miss Moneypenny, secretary to James Bond's boss M – the Moneypenny character was originally called "Petty" Petteval. Possibly it was through her that Fleming came across Thomson's book.

Thomson's writing was of sufficiently high calibre to prompt Dorothy L. Sayers to heap praise on Richardson's performance in his third case: "he puts in some of that excellent, sober, straightforward detective work which he so well knows how to do and follows the clue of a post-mark to the heart of a very plausible and proper mystery. I find him a most agreeable companion." The acerbic American critics Jacques Barzun and Wendell

Hertig Taylor also had a soft spot for Richardson, saying in *A Catalogue of Crime* that his investigations amount to "early police routine minus the contrived bickering, stomach ulcers, and pub-crawling with which later writers have masked poverty of invention and the dullness of repetitive questioning".

Books in the Richardson series have been out of print and hard to find for decades, and their reappearance at affordable prices is as welcome as it is overdue. Now that Dean Street Press have republished all eight recorded entries in the Richardson case-book, twenty-first century readers are likely to find his company just as agreeable as Sayers did.

Martin Edwards

www.martinedwardsbooks.com

Chapter One

DIVISIONAL DETECTIVE-INSPECTOR SYMINGTON was checking the expense sheets of his men in his little barely furnished room at the Hampstead Police Station when the telephone rang. He jerked a thumb in the direction of the instrument without speaking, and his clerk went to it, leaving him free to wrestle with columns of figures. Arithmetic, as all his staff knew, had never been his strong suit. He had a pathetic habit of doing his addition sums aloud, and he was thus engaged when phrases in the one-sided telephone conversation caught his ear and he broke away from his brain-torture to listen.

"Spell the name, please. M-a-c-D-o-u-g-a-l—MacDougal... Yes, Mr. MacDougal?...You think she was murdered?...Has any doctor seen her?...Oh, a window was open?...You think he got in and went out through the window? Well, stay where you are, and whatever you do, don't touch the body or anything else until an officer comes. Stop, don't go away...Have I got your address right?—23 Laburnum Road. Is that right? Very good, Mr. MacDougal—an officer will be at the house within ten minutes."

Symington pushed back his papers and started to his feet. Burglary and murder were matters that he understood better than columns of figures. He listened with impatience to the level voice of his subordinate while he recounted the substance of the telephone message. "Are any of the men back?" he asked.

His clerk opened the door into the adjoining room and glanced in. "Only Porter, sir. He's writing his report on that house-breaking case in Claremont Terrace."

Symington went to the peg for his hat. "I'll go myself. Make a note of the name and address for me: tell Porter to come along with me, and while we are gone, repeat the message to C.O." By these initials he meant the Central Office at New Scotland Yard.

It was the practice in that grim building for telephone messages reporting serious crimes from a Division to be brought down by one of the operators upstairs to the Chief Constable's messenger, and if that functionary happened to be otherwise engaged, to hand it to one of the detective-sergeants to speed it on its way to the proper authority. It chanced that the only man in the sergeants' room that morning was Detective-Sergeant Richardson, a young Scotsman, whose rise from a uniform constable to a detective-sergeant had led to some grumbling from colleagues over whose head he had passed. It would have led to more if he had been less popular. But being, as he was, one of those young men who never pushed himself forward, nor attempted to take credit for his successes even when the credit was due, he disarmed hostile criticism.

"Here's something for you to get on with, Richardson," said the telephone operator, planking the message down on his desk.

"Another daylight raid?"

"Not this time. It's a murder up in Hampstead. The D.D.I. is on the job. A report's following."

Richardson read the message and sighed. A plain-sailing murder case in one of the divisions was unlikely to come his way. For weeks he had been condemned to interview indignant ladies who had written in to complain that their handbags had been snatched from them in broad daylight, in several cases only to find a little later that they had left them lying on the counter of the last shop they had visited; or to pacify imaginative persons of both sexes who were convinced that they were being shadowed by members of a criminal gang. The least humdrum job that had come his way during the last few weeks had been to squeeze himself into an office cupboard a size too small for him to listen to the threats of a blackmailer who imagined that he was alone with his victim.

He read the message—that at 11.13 a.m. James MacDougal of 23 Laburnum Road, Hampstead, had telephoned to the Hampstead Police Station to report that on reaching home at 11 a.m. he had found the front door locked and bolted; that he rang repeatedly without effect and then went round to the back, where he found a window open. In the kitchen the gas-oven was alight: it had burnt a hole through the saucepan over it; the table was laid for the maid's supper. On going up to the hall above he found the body of his maidservant, Helen Dunn, aged about fifty, lying on the floor near the telephone. She had bled profusely from a wound in the head and her body was cold. D.D. Inspector Symington and P.C. Porter (C.I.D.) have left for the scene of the crime.

Richardson carried the message to the Chief Constable's room.

"What is it?" growled Beckett, who was wading through a thick file of papers and jotting down notes as he read.

"A case of house-breaking and murder in Hampstead, sir. D.D. Inspector Symington is now at the house."

Beckett put out his hand for the message, glanced at it, initialed it and threw it into his basket before resuming his work. From that basket it would go automatically to Morden, the Deputy Assistant Commissioner, and from him to Sir William Lorimer. As Richardson knew, no action would be taken by Headquarters until Symington's report was received.

No. 23 Laburnum Road was a square, ugly Victorian house standing in its own garden; a semi-circular carriage drive led from the gate to the front door. In answer to Symington's ring the door was opened instantly. "I am Divisional Detective-Inspector Symington from Hampstead Police Station," he announced. "I have had your telephone message. You are Mr. MacDougal?"

"Yes, that is my name. I'm very glad you've come. This terrible affair has been a great shock to me."

Symington required no corroboration of that statement: the old man was pale and his mouth was twitching. He was a tall, spare man with stooping shoulders and dreamy eyes that seemed short-sighted, and he looked like a professor of some kind—the sort of man who is ill-fitted to deal with the hard facts of life. In fact, as Symington came afterwards to know, he was one of those stay-at-home archaeologists who make a hobby of the modern excavations in Palestine and their bearing on the Jewish history of the Pentateuch; a F.S.A. who attended every meeting of the Society and occasionally took part in the discussions.

The first step to be taken was to summon the police surgeon to examine the body, which was lying on the floor only three feet from the table on which the telephone stood: indeed, when Porter went to the instrument, he had to step over the body and avoid treading on the patch of coagulated blood which had flowed from the head. Symington did not touch the body: he asked MacDougal to show him the window which he had found open when he came home. He was taken down stone steps to the kitchen. There, as had already been reported on the telephone, he saw that a saucepan of aluminium which was standing on the gas-stove had been split open by the heat and partly melted.

"You found the gas still burning when you came in this morning?"

"Yes, and I turned it off. The gas-tap was the only thing I touched, except the door of my library. Naturally I had to see that my books and manuscripts were safe."

"You found the front door bolted on the inside?"

"Yes, my latch-key wouldn't open it. I went round the house and found that window open, and I climbed in."

The contents of the saucepan had burned into black, greasy ash, but some of the liquid had boiled over, and it was easy to gather from the dried stains on the stove that it had been cocoa. There was no sign of any struggle in the kitchen: everything was tidy and scrupulously clean. But the lower half of the window had been pushed up; one of its upper panes was broken. Symington took out a reading-glass and examined the pane, especially near the fracture; then he leaned out to examine the flowerbed underneath. There were footprints in the soft earth—the prints of boots. Mentally he made a preliminary reconstruction of the crime. The maid had been preparing her supper at the stove with her back to the window when the window-pane had been smashed with a hammer or a stone, leaving an aperture wide enough to admit a hand to draw back the catch. Probably the dead woman had screamed, but the nearest house was too distant for the cry to have been heard. Then, seeing a man getting in through the window, she had run upstairs to telephone for help, but before she could reach the instrument he had overtaken her and killed her by some means which it would be the police surgeon's business to determine. He invited MacDougal to sit down and answer a few questions while they were waiting for the doctor.

"You were away when this happened?"

"Yes, I had to attend the funeral of my brother-in-law at Redford."

"What was his name?"

"Thomas Ilford. My sister wrote to tell me that he had left me executor to his will—sole executor."

"He had property to leave?"

"Yes, he owned a good deal of house property in Redford as well as invested money."

"What time did you leave home?"

"It must have been a few minutes after nine. I had to catch the ten-thirty train."

"Your servant did not mind being left alone in this big house?"

"No, but she was not going to be alone all night. My nephew landed at Portsmouth the day before yesterday, and was coming to stay with me. He was really not due until to-day, but I sent him an express letter asking him to come and sleep here last night."

"His name?" (Symington was taking notes.)

"Ronald Eccles."

"Is he still serving, or has he retired?"

"He's still serving. His ship is the *Dauntless*, just back from the West Indies to refit."

"Had you any particular reason for asking him to come a day earlier?"

"Well, yes, I had. There was a considerable sum of money in the house in Treasury notes—two thousand seven hundred and fifty pounds to be exact."

"As much as that? Do you always keep such large amounts in the house?"

"Certainly not. It worried me, but there was no way out of it. You see, I had just sold a dairy farm to the tenant who had rented it for years. You know what these farmers are. They don't trust banks, but keep their money in an old stocking."

"The farmer's name?"

"Edward Jackson."

"And the name of the farm you sold?"

"Two Ways Farm. That is the name in the title deeds and the Ordnance Survey, but everyone in Redford knows it as 'Jackson's Farm.'"

"And this Mr. Jackson paid you in cash for it? Why did he not pay the money to your lawyer in Redford?"

"I can't answer that question. The old man was very anxious, he said, to complete the sale, and he doesn't trust lawyers any more than he trusts bankers. He wanted to pay the money and get my receipt for it, so he did not waste money on a telegram. He got my letter accepting his offer for the farm on Monday morning, and he arrived here on Monday afternoon at four o'clock—too late for me to pay the money into my bank."

"Why didn't you pay it in yesterday morning before you went to Redford for the funeral?"

"Because I couldn't be in two places at once. If I had waited until the bank opened I should have been too late for the funeral, and that would have distressed my poor sister terribly. I did the next best thing. I have no safe in the house, so I hid the money and wrote an express letter to my nephew telling him to come up yesterday and sleep in the house last night, instead of coming up to-day as he intended."

"Did you tell him the reason?"

"Yes, and I told him where the money was. I took the letter to the Hampstead Post Office myself and expressed it. He must have received it yesterday morning."

"But he didn't come?"

"Apparently not. I suppose that he had difficulty about getting leave. But it was unlike him not to telegraph and say so."

"How did you address the letter?"

"To his ship, the *Dauntless*, in Portsmouth Dock."

"Where did you hide the money?"

"In my bedroom."

"But where?"

"In a chest of drawers, under my clothes."

"And you found it all right?"

"I haven't been upstairs to look yet."

"You haven't *looked*?" Symington's tone showed his astonishment.

"No. In the face of the awful thing that's happened I did not give a thought to the money. I suppose it was the shock."

"This must be cleared up at once, Mr. MacDougal. We'll go upstairs and see whether the money is in the place where you hid it. You lead the way."

They passed through the hall where Porter was standing on guard over the body, and went upstairs to a bedroom on the first floor. MacDougal recoiled with an exclamation when he opened the door. The room was in confusion. The drawers in the chest had been pulled out and were lying on the floor, which was littered with clothing. MacDougal began a feverish search among the litter, kneeling on the floor, the better to assure himself that the precious bag was not lying under the pile of clothes. He rose and faced Symington. "It's no use digging any further at that pile. It's gone."

"You mean the money you hid in one of those drawers? Are you quite sure?"

"Yes," he said in a hopeless tone. "It's gone."

"Was it enclosed in a box?"

"No, it was in a dirty calico bag, just as the farmer brought it to me. I counted it over with him and gave him a receipt. I tied up the bag with the same string and hid it under my clothes in the bottom drawer and locked the drawer."

"Then let us get the drawers back and you can show me exactly where you hid it. Quick, or the doctor may be here before we've finished."

It was the best treatment for frayed nerves. The old man fell to work. When the drawers were back in their places MacDougal pointed to the centre of the bottom drawer at the back.

"This drawer was packed with clothes, inspector. It was a tight fit to get the drawer shut." He lugged a bunch of keys from his trouser pocket. "I locked every drawer with this key, but you see what the man did—forced the locks of all three drawers! "

It was true. The chest, which purported to be solid mahogany, was a sham; the mahogany was thinly veneered on deal; the locks were cheap and were secured to the wood by inadequate little screws; a sharp jerk on the handles had sufficed to tear out the topmost screws, and the locks were hanging useless by their bottom screws. Symington cast an eye round the room and went to a cupboard. It was locked: nothing else in the room appeared to have been touched.

"Listen to me, Mr. MacDougal. How many people knew that the money was in that drawer? Did your servant know?"

"Certainly not. If I had given her a hint that there was so much money in the house, she would have refused to stay the night here. She was very independent, poor thing. She would have gone off to spend the night with her married sister in Hammersmith."

"Did the farmer, Jackson, know?"

"No, I told him nothing. All he wanted was for me to count the money in his presence, get a receipt and be off."

"But you told your nephew?"

"Yes, because I had to give him a good reason for coming up a day earlier."

"Tell me exactly what you said in your letter."

"I can't say that I remember the exact words I used. I told him that Jackson had called after banking hours on Monday and had paid over the money; I told him the amount and said that I should have to leave for the funeral in Redford before the bank opened on Tuesday, and that it wouldn't do to leave my maidservant alone in the house with such a sum lying in a drawer; that I had no safe in the house to put it in. I begged him to come up one day earlier so as to sleep in the house."

"You didn't tell him the exact hiding-place?"

"No, I'm certain of that."

"And you are quite certain that you didn't tell anyone else. Think before you answer."

"I'm quite certain."

A bell rang faintly in the basement. The inspector pricked up his ears. "What bell was that?"

"The front-door bell, I think."

Symington went to the door to listen. He heard Porter go to the front door and the voice of the visitor, which sounded familiar.

"It is the police surgeon, Mr. MacDougal. I must go down, but you can stay here or come down with me, whichever you wish."

"I would rather come down."

Symington greeted the newcomer as "Dr. Macnamara." He was a stout little man of about forty, with an air of business about him. He put his attaché-case on the hall table. "What have you got for me to-day, Mr. Symington?"

"If you'll look behind you, Doctor, you'll see."

"Tck, tck!" clicked the doctor, going down on hands and knees beside the body and gently turning it over, giving special attention to the head. They let him work in silence for some minutes. Then he rose and faced Symington.

"This woman has been shot through the head from behind, and the bullet passed clean through the skull. The shot must have been fired at close quarters. You can see that from the clean point of entry at the back of the head and the mess it made of the forehead at the point of exit. If you look about you ought to be able to find the bullet."

"The man who fired the shot got in through the kitchen window. He must have run after her up the basement stairs and fired at her from about where I am standing," said Symington.

"Ah, then I should look for the bullet in that wall."

"I think I see it, sir," said Porter. "Here, where I am pointing, there is a hole in the plaster."

Symington hurried over to him and pulled out his knife. After a few seconds' probing he prised out something that fell on the boards. It was a small bullet slightly flattened by its impact against the wall. Porter slipped it into an envelope and labelled it.

"Now, Mr. Symington, you can 'phone for the ambulance and get the body down to the mortuary for the post-mortem, while I get back to finish my lunch, if you don't mind."

"Very good, Doctor: it shall be done. Ring up the station for the ambulance, Porter, and then come down with me to the kitchen. We won't trouble you any more for the present, Mr. MacDougal, but don't go out."

When Porter reached the kitchen after sending his message he found the room empty and the back door open. His chief came in from the garden.

"I want you to get through to the Portsmouth Dockyard police on the trunk—Portsmouth 356 is the number. Ask them to send round to H.M.S. *Dauntless* and inquire whether Lieutenant

Eccles is on board, and if not, at what time he left the ship. Tell them to telephone their report to our office."

While his subordinate was wrestling with the trunk call, Symington betook himself to the garden again in the hope of finding some clue to the number of persons who had made a felonious entry overnight. It would be easy, of course, to compare the soles of MacDougal's boots with the booted footprints: it might be well to get a photograph of the others before a shower of rain obliterated their outlines. Symington walked round towards the entrance gate and made a cast into the laurel bushes on his left. His heart beat fast when five yards from the drive he came upon a laurel leaf, fresh-plucked, lying on the ground, and close to it a clear footprint.

He stepped back into the drive and looked towards the house. Porter had come out. He seemed to be looking for him. Symington waved an arm and the man came to him, almost at a run.

"Did you get through to them all right?"

"Yes, sir. They told me—"

"You can tell me that later. I want you to look at this." He led his subordinate to the footprint. "A pretty clear print that, wouldn't you say? We'll take a cast from it presently, but in the meantime I want you to measure it carefully."

"Very good, sir. I don't know whether you've noticed how thin the sole is. It looks like the kind of shoe that gentlemen wear in town. Oh, and here's another."

"H'm! It's the same shoe all right, but I doubt whether it's clear enough for a cast."

"I'm afraid not, sir, but the man who made it must have been walking away from the drive, because here's another. And look there, sir!" Porter was pointing to something lying on the ground: he pounced on it and passed it to his chief. It was a black leather pocket-book or note-case.

Symington opened it eagerly. The flaps were full of memoranda scribbled on slips of paper, a letter or two, and—biggest prize of all—three or four visiting-cards.

"Look at this, Porter." He handed him one of the visiting-cards bearing the name "Mr. Ronald Eccles," and in the left lower corner—"H.M.S. *Dauntless*."

"This is something like a clue, sir."

Chapter Two

THERE WAS a difference of opinion in high quarters at New Scotland Yard when Symington brought down the report of his visit to Laburnum Road. Charles Morden and Chief Constable Beckett did not see eye to eye on the question whether the inquiry should be put into the hands of one of the superintendents or left in the quite competent hands of Divisional Detective-Inspector Symington.

"He's begun quite well," said Beckett. "Why take it out of his hands? I should let him go through with-it. They're having a quiet time in S Division just now."

Morden fell back upon the tradition that whenever a case entailed work in several divisions of the Metropolitan area, or help was to be invoked from provincial police forces, a superintendent or a chief inspector from the Central Division was the man to undertake the case; and further, that if some public official was involved (and a naval officer came under the head of a public official), it was the immemorial practice for Central to handle the case. "You see," he said, "this may grow into a big case when the newspapers get hold of the details. A naval officer's pocket-book found on the scene of the crime! The naval officer on leave at the time. How did the pocket-book get there? I've just been looking through its contents. Besides the visiting-cards and the letters in feminine handwritings, there is the very letter which the uncle sent by express to his ship. I don't suppose you've had time to read it. Just run your eye over it."

Beckett went through the letter with knitted brow, murmuring its contents aloud.

"DEAR RONALD,

"I am delighted to hear that you are back and that you are coming to me for a few days—as you say—to 'refit.' I am much looking forward to your visit, my dear boy, but I want you to make a slight modification in your dates. I want you here to-morrow (Tuesday) instead of Wednesday for a very special reason. I think I told you that Jackson of Two Ways Farm was worrying me to let him buy the farm outright. After a lot of haggling he agreed to my price, and this afternoon, instead of going to Pringle, my Redford lawyer, the old fool turned up here with a bag stuffed full of Treasury notes. It was too late for the bank, and I have to start for Redford to attend poor Harry Winter's funeral before the bank opens to-morrow morning and I can't get back before Wednesday at about eleven.

"So I, too, have been driven to the stocking method of hoarding! I've had to hide the money-bag under the clothes in my chest of drawers under lock and key, and trust to no one knowing about it except you. If poor old Helen knew that she was to be left alone in the house with nearly £3,000 to guard, she'd bolt, and then good-bye to that cunning pastry of hers to which you have been looking forward.

"Seriously, my dear boy, I do want you to come and sleep in the house to-morrow night *without fail*. It will make my mind much easier. It is easier already because I feel sure that you will.

"Yours ever,

"UNCLE JIM."

Beckett handed the letter back and went to the window to think. "The captain of the *Dauntless* told the dockyard people that the nephew got leave on urgent private affairs and left the ship early on Tuesday morning. If he took the next train, he ought to have been in London by lunch-time. It's funny. And then his pocket-book is picked up in the garden on the morning after the murder! And no one has seen or heard of him since! But so far there's nothing in the case that Symington couldn't handle. He's started with the advantage of knowing MacDougal and the house and grounds, and he's a regular ferret for getting to the bottom of his cases."

"He is, but when he comes to a sticking-point, as he's bound to, we shall be made to take over the case in Central, so why not begin now? Probably there'll be questions in the House, and the Home Office people will want to know who's in charge of the case. We shall have to get the inquest adjourned—"

"Oh, that needn't worry us. Symington is on the best of terms with the Hampstead coroner—"

"No doubt he is, but—well, talking won't make either of us change our opinion: we shall have to ask Sir William to decide."

Morden touched his desk telephone and had an answering buzz.

"Are you very busy? Beckett and I want you to decide a point that has arisen in this Hampstead murder case...Right! We'll come."

The two passed through the swing doors of the entrance hall to a room facing the granite staircase. The Office of Works, with a fine sense of the differences of rank in the hierarchy, had furnished it more lavishly than any other room on the ground floor. It had, for example, a Turkey carpet and mahogany furniture. On the big writing-table in the centre was a miniature telephone exchange, with private wires connected with the various Government departments. At this table sat Sir William Lorimer, the Director of Criminal Investigation, an intelligent-looking person of about fifty with an easy manner and a sense of humour.

"Good morning, both of you. I gather that you were on the point of coming to blows when you rang me up. What's the trouble?"

"It's about that murder in Hampstead," explained Morden with a wry smile. "You've seen the telephone messages?"

"The murder of the servant in Laburnum Road?"

"Yes. We want you to decide whether the case should be taken over by Central. Mr. Beckett thinks that it should be left to the Division."

"Didn't I see that a naval officer was somehow involved in the case?"

"Yes, but only to the extent that his pocket-book was picked up in the garden. There's nothing yet to show that he dropped it there."

Beckett remained silent, being one of those men who are loath to give their opinion until it is asked for.

"What do you say, Mr. Beckett?" asked Lorimer.

"Well, sir, I'm in favour of leaving it to the Divisional Detective-Inspector. Mr. Symington is a very careful man and he knows his division inside out. He's already begun the case, and I don't see why he shouldn't go through with it. S Division is pretty free from crime at the moment, though of course at this season it's had its share of burglaries and house-breaking."

"I'm afraid that I must rule against you, Mr. Beckett. It is just one of those cases in which I shall be pestered with questions, and I want to feel that I've only to ring the bell to get a quick answer; whereas, if the inquiry is going on in Hampstead—But please understand that I've every confidence in Symington, and that if it had been an ordinary case, however difficult, I should have said, 'Leave it in his hands.' Which of the superintendents is free at this moment?"

"Only Foster can be spared at present, Sir William."

"Very well, then, let Foster take it on. He may be a bit slow, but he's sure, and his Scottish accent gives one confidence somehow." He turned to Morden. "You'd better send for him and put him in charge of the case. Let him choose the man to work with him."

Beckett permitted himself to laugh sardonically. Lorimer looked up in surprise.

What are you laughing at, Mr. Beckett?"

Well, sir, I was thinking that I knew who he'd choose—that new second-class sergeant in Central— Sergeant Richardson."

"Well, I don't know that we could do better. They make a good team."

Thus the junior superintendent and the junior of the detective-sergeants in Central found themselves engaged on a case that was destined to prove far-reaching in its consequences. Charles Morden sent for Foster and gave him all the papers to read. "Sir William wishes you to take over this case, Mr. Foster. It may turn out to be an important case. Who would you like to take with you?"

Foster's blue eyes narrowed. "I'd rather have Sergeant Richardson, sir."

"Why not a more senior man?" asked Morden with a twinkle in his eye.

"Well, sir, I suppose that it's because he knows my way of working and—the man's got ideas."

"Very well; Sir William said that you were to choose your own man. You'd better go carefully through this file, paying special attention to the enclosures in that pocket-book before you visit the scene of the crime. You will find in it two letters that seem to show that Lieutenant Eccles was in urgent need of money. The first is from a moneylender, threatening to complain to the Admiralty unless a loan of seventy pounds is at once repaid, and another from a woman which is getting very near blackmail. Here it is: I'll read it to you. She gives no address and only dates the letter 'Thursday.'

'DEAR RONNY,

   'I am sorry to have to write a plain-spoken letter to you, but the time has gone past for pretty speeches. Unless I have £200 by return of post we shall be in the soup, and will have to let the farm go for what it will fetch. I was a fool to listen to your pretty speeches: if I hadn't listened to you I should have been rolling in money now, but you barged in and spoilt everything and now I've no one to look to but you. Don't say that you can't raise the money somehow, because I know you can. You've spoilt my life, and the least you can do is to make amends. If you want us to keep on the farm send the money by return. If I don't get it in time it will be the end. You'll live to regret it.

                         'Yours,

                                   'GWEN.'

What do you make of that?"

"It scarcely reads like a blackmailing letter, sir, but until we can get an explanation from Lieutenant Eccles himself, it is impossible to say what were his relations with the writer. The first thing is to find him."

"Quite so, but these two letters show that he was in urgent need of money, and the finding of his pocket-book in the garden, coupled with his disappearance, are making things look rather black. Symington has already started on the case, but I dare say that he won't be sorry to be relieved of it. I'll ring him up and tell him that Central will take it over and why. When you've gone through the papers you'd better run up to Hampstead and get him to take you down to the house. Let me have the file back before you go. Sir William hasn't seen it yet."

"You shall have it in half an hour, sir."

Foster had an uncanny knack of mastering the contents of a file and storing the salient facts in his memory in a few minutes. In twenty minutes the file was back on Morden's table and he was half-way to Hampstead in the Tube. The neatly dressed young man beside him was Sergeant Richardson: the other passengers would have thought them unacquainted, for they said not a word to one another until they were clear of the Tube station.

"You've never met D.D. Inspector Symington, have you, Richardson?"

"No, sir."

"He's one of the best thief-catchers in the service. Have you ever come across the detective patrol, Porter?"

"Yes, sir. He went through the detective class with me."

"Good! Then while I'm having a talk with the D.D. Inspector, you might do worse than have a yarn with him and see what he thinks of the case. He was the officer who accompanied Mr. Symington to the house."

"Very well, sir, I will, if we're lucky enough to find him in the office."

Having been warned by telephone that Foster was on his way to Hampstead, Symington was in his room and Porter had been warned to be in the sergeants' room in case he should be wanted. If Foster was in any doubt about the quality of his reception by the man he was supplanting in the case, it was at once set at rest. "I'm very glad that you're taking this case over, Mr. Foster," said Symington; "it promises to be a very ticklish case and I haven't men enough here to undertake all the inquiries without neglecting cases in my own division. You have read my report?

Is there anything you would like to ask me before you go on to the house?"

"Yes, I want to talk the case over with you and get your personal impressions." Thereupon they engaged in a long discussion.

Meanwhile Richardson had looked into the room where the sergeants were at work on their reports and had found Porter, his old classmate. After exchanging greetings, he told him that the murder case had been taken over by Superintendent Foster of Central, who was in conference with Mr. Symington at that moment. "It's going to be a tough nut to crack, don't you think?"

"It all depends how soon we get that nephew," observed Porter. "You may get some sense out of *him*."

"You don't think the uncle told you the whole story?"

"Good Lord, no! He couldn't tell a connected story—not if it was to save him from the gallows. He's one of these vapouring professor-chaps. All this stuff about the money hidden in a drawer! He's the sort of feller that is always waking out of a dream—the sort that would accuse you of stealing his watch and come along two days later to say that he was sorry to have caused any trouble, but he'd found the watch on his dressing-table when he got home. You'll get nothing coherent out of *him*."

Symington looked in and beckoned to Richardson, who found Foster ready to start for Laburnum Road. The two seniors walked ahead, deep in conversation: Richardson followed a few paces behind, taking keen note of the streets through which they passed. Arrived at the gate of No. 23, Foster turned to him and said, "Three of us will be too many for Mr. MacDougal, I think. You had better play about in the garden, Richardson, until I call you in." As the two seniors went up the drive, Symington took Foster a few steps into the laurels to show him the spot where he had found the pocket-book and the footprints.

"I suppose that we'd better take casts of the footprints?" said Foster.

"Yes. I haven't had time to get it done myself."

When the front door had closed behind the two seniors, Richardson began to "play about in the garden." It was a sedate game. Beside the drive were two long and narrow rose-beds, and something in them attracted his close attention. It was a deeply indented footprint in the soft earth. He pulled out his pocket diary in which he recorded the weather conditions day by day. It had not rained since the night of the murder. Now, even a jobbing gardener does not plant his foot on a flower-bed, or if he has occasion to do so, he smooths over the defacement with a rake. A few feet farther on was a print of the same foot: the toes of both pointed towards the house. He crossed to the bed on the other side of the drive, and there, not only did he find a print of the same boot, but two of them with the toes pointing towards the next house. There were other marks between them: a branch of the standard rose had been broken and was hanging to the stem by a shred of bark, and six feet farther on was a print of the same boot with the toe pointing in the opposite direction. Suddenly the explanation flashed on him: the footprints were those of a drunken man aiming for the front door. He had lurched off the drive into the rose-bed on the right and had then staggered across the gravel into the bed on the other side, colliding with the standard rose and falling. The fall accounted for the other marks in the earth. Then he picked himself up and got back into the drive, where his feet left no impression. Richardson went back to the footprints and went down on his knees to examine them more closely. The boots that had made them were not such as townsmen wear: the heels were shod with iron, and the tip of the iron horseshoe on the right heel had been broken off at one of its screw-holes. That might prove to be a useful clue hereafter.

He went round to the back of the house to look at the footprints under the broken kitchen window. They, too, had lain undisturbed, though the earth had dried in the wind. Here the difficulty was to know which had been made by the owner of the house: all seemed to have been made by gentlemen's walking-shoes. The country-made boots of the drunken man had made no impression here. Richardson tried to reconstruct the movements of the inebriated visitor. He had been making for the front door: he reached it and rang the bell, or plied the knocker. No one came, because the only person left in the house was a dead woman. So this visitor arrived not before, but after the murder. Had the farmer who had paid over the money gone off and made a night of it, and come back with some confused idea of getting his money back? Could it have been his visit that had so alarmed the murderer that he left everything in confusion?

He turned to the window, pulled from his pocket a little tin box containing two tiny, wide-mouthed bottles, the one with black and the other a white powder, and a camel-hair brush. Dipping this into the white powder, he passed the brush gently over the glass surrounding the fracture, without result. Undiscouraged, he repeated the process over both the lower panes, and here his patience was rewarded: a thumb or fingerprint flashed out like the image on an exposed negative under the developer, as soon as he had blown away the superfluous powder. He examined it through a glass: it was a disappointing impression, for the pressure of the finger that had made it had slipped, and the ridges were blurred. He blew the white powder from the brush and dipped it into the black powder. Reflecting that a man who lifts the sash of a window uses his thumbs under the sash-bar to push it up, he painted the underside of the sash-bar with black, and blew off the superfluity. Here he was successful beyond his hopes. Two perfect thumb-prints stood out on the white paint. It was at that moment of triumph that Foster opened the back door and found him.

"Oh, there you are! I've been looking for you all over the place."

"I'm sorry, sir. I've been looking about and I've found a good fingerprint on the window-frame."

"The devil you have! Let me have a look at it. Yes, it's a print all right, but short of taking out the window-frame, how are we to get it photographed?"

"If I fix the impression first, Mr. Foster, we can easily take out the window and get it boarded up. We could even take it into court as an exhibit. Juries like that kind of exhibit."

"Go ahead then and fix it, as you seem to be one of those fingerprint fiends."

Richardson took this as a compliment. In his spare time he had chummed up with one of the sergeants in the fingerprint department, who had pointed him out to Wilkins, the superintendent, as a likely recruit for the section: indeed, Superintendent Wilkins had actually sounded him on the question, but as there was no vacancy at the moment, the proposal had gone no further than lending him a manual to read and giving him desultory instruction. Richardson had sat up at nights delving into a science that fascinated him, and had pored over the exhibits of past cases in which fingerprints had played a deciding role. It was true that Wilkins had warned him against building too much upon prints found on the scene of a crime to the neglect of other evidence, from which almost equally sound deductions could be drawn. He had said, "You've always got to remember, my boy, that out of the thousands of crimes committed in the metropolitan area every year, we get only a dozen in which a print found on the scene of a crime is the only piece of evidence. Then, of course, we make a song about it, because the ignorant public, from which jurymen are drawn, needs educating. Most of the prints left by burglars and safe-breakers are useless for our purpose because they are blurred; others are useless because the men who left their prints behind them had never been convicted before and therefore their prints were not in our files; and lastly, experienced burglars are alive to the danger they run, and before they set out to break in, they buy a pair of gloves."

"But those cases, sir!" objected Richardson, pointing to photographs of successes displayed on the wall.

"The list is a pretty small one. You must remember that until last year we couldn't make a classification from the print of a single finger. We arrived at the classification largely by guesswork. Now, things promise to be better, because one of my sergeants has been ingenious enough to devise a system of classification from a single finger, but his system has still to be tried out. When those prints over there were enlarged and photographed, we had to begin by guessing which of the ten fingers made the print. Suppose it was a loop: then we had to use the rule of average frequency to guess what the patterns on the other fingers were likely to be if this kind of loop belonged to the first finger of the right hand. Having done that, we made an experimental classification and went to the appropriate pigeon-hole. If we failed to find it there we had to start all over again."

"There was that case at Deptford, sir."

"You mean the case where the man left his whole finger on a spike of the gate as he was getting over. Poor devil! The spike caught in his ring as he was jumping down. That happened to be an easy case because we knew which finger it was, but we made a stir about it because it happened in the early days of the system and we wanted to educate the public. In that case, of course, we had corroborative evidence in the fact that when the man was arrested that finger was missing from his left hand: we had it here in a bottle of spirits and had taken a print from it. He was an old hand at the game of warehouse-breaking."

"If the print is in the collection at all, you always find it in the end?"

"I would not like to go as far as that. We may fail sometimes, but not very often, I fancy. The search may take five minutes, or it may take a couple of days, and sometimes, perhaps, it beats us. It is possible that we may have reported that a print is not in the collection when it was there all the time, but I don't remember such a case."

"Of course the man who made the print may not be the burglar at all."

"Quite true, and that is the reason for our rule that whenever such a fingerprint is brought in, the officer who brings it must submit to having his own fingerprints taken before we begin our search. I remember a case some years ago in which an inspector from the West of England brought me a polished stone axe from the local museum, which had been broken into. There was a beautiful fingerprint on it, but when we came to take the inspector's fingerprints, I was able to show him that it was the impression of his own thumb! He didn't seem to like it, but it saved us a lot of useless work. If, in the course of your work, you come across a good fingerprint, by all means bring it along, but make sure first that it isn't your own, or that of one of your colleagues in the case."

Bearing this advice in mind, Richardson took from his pocket a little scent spray containing the fixative used by artists for fixing charcoal drawings, and sprayed the two prints on the sash-bar. Foster watched the operation with amused curiosity.

"One would think that you were one of Superintendent Wilkins' young men, Richardson. I must look out, or he'll be tempting you to leave me."

"No fear of that, Mr. Foster. I'm only doing what they taught us in the detective class. Now, if you don't mind, I should like to take your prints as a precaution. You may have touched this window."

"I might, if I had been near it, but I haven't. What you'll have to do is to take the fingerprints of Mr. Symington and the gentleman upstairs—Mr. MacDougal—but that can very well wait. What we've got to do now—"

"Excuse me for interrupting you, sir, but I've found something else." He described the footprints of the drunken man he had found in the rose-beds bordering on the drive. Foster went with him to look at them.

"With your permission, sir, I should like to take a plaster cast of this footprint. You see the heelplate on the boot is broken."

"It might be worth while, though the man who murdered that woman couldn't have been drunk when he shot her. A cast of the footprint couldn't lead to much, and it would waste valuable time if you go off to buy plaster of Paris and things."

"It won't take five minutes, sir; I have the stuff with me."

"Good Lord, Richardson. Is there anything you haven't brought with you in that bag of yours? Well, go ahead."

Richardson opened his attaché-case and took out a paper bag containing plaster of Paris. He took off his coat and ran off to the kitchen, returning with a jug of water and a handful of straw from a wine-case. He broke straws to fit the length and breadth of the footprint, ran the powdered plaster into the jug, stirred it vigorously with a stick, and as soon as it was of the consistency of cream, poured a thin layer into the footprint and laid the straws on it. Then he continued pouring until the footprint was full to overflowing. He packed up his things and put on his coat.

"Now, sir, we can leave it to set. I'll just run back with the jug and wash it out, or Mr. MacDougal's new servant will be complaining, and then I'll be ready."

Foster gazed at his retreating form with an amused smile. He was thinking that his subordinate would go far in his profession. As Richardson was returning at a run, a young man of medium height pushed back the gate and came in. There was a proprietary air about him as he advanced up the drive.

"What's all this?" he asked. "What are you men doing here?"

"I'm a superintendent from Scotland Yard, sir," replied Foster. "May I ask you your name?"

"I'm Ronald Eccles, a lieutenant in the Royal Navy."

Chapter Three

IF SUPERINTENDENT FOSTER was startled at the apparition of a young man who was in a position, as he thought, to clear up the mystery, he did not show it. "We've been looking for you, Mr. Eccles," he said.

"The devil you have? What's it all about? Nothing's happened to my uncle, I hope?"

"You know that there was a burglary here on Tuesday night?"

"A burglary? You're joking?" Foster and Richardson were watching his face. If his astonishment and dismay were assumed, both decided that he was a loss to the stage of melodrama. "Did the burglars get away with anything?"

"With a large sum of money, we understand, but instead of standing here to talk I should be glad if you would come into the house with us and let me take a statement from you."

"All right—though I don't see that I can tell you anything useful." He began to lead the way to the front door.

"Not that way, sir, if you don't mind. We'll go round to the kitchen for our interview. This way, sir."

"But I want to see my uncle first. Then I'll answer as many questions as you like to ask, and I'll ask you a few in return."

"I'm sorry, sir. Your uncle is quite well and you shall see him in good time, but you will kindly do as I say, and come with me to the kitchen." The claws had begun to peep out from under the velvet glove.

"Oh, very well—if you're so damned particular. Go ahead and let us get it over."

They walked round the angle of the house, Richardson bringing up the rear with his attaché-case from which he abstracted a reporter's note-book as he went. His shorthand was not impeccable, but with occasional recourse to abbreviated longhand, aided by a good memory, he had found it equal to the task of taking down a statement. The three sat down at the kitchen table.

"Your name is Ronald Eccles," began Foster; "a lieutenant in His Majesty's Navy. What is your age?"

"Twenty-six."

"What ship are you serving on?"

"The *Dauntless*, but she's in dock now."

"In dock at Portsmouth. When did you leave her?"

"Between nine and ten on Tuesday." The replies were given sharply as if under protest.

Foster seemed to receive the last answer with surprise.

"On *Tuesday*, and this is Thursday. Your uncle expected you here on Tuesday, to spend the night here. What were you doing in the meantime?"

"You may well ask me that. I've had a hell of a time."

"Where have you been? You had better give me an account of all your movements."

"I don't think that you have any right to ask. You are behaving as if I was under suspicion of something. Tell me what's behind all this and then I'll decide whether I ought to submit to this questioning."

"All in good time, Mr. Eccles. I am sure that as a naval officer you don't want to obstruct me in my duty. It is my duty to ask you to account for all your movements after you left the ship."

"I don't want to obstruct you. I was going to complain to the police in any case. The first thing I did on leaving the ship was to taxi out of the town to see a friend."

"What was the name of the friend and his address?"

"I'm not bound to give you that."

"May I take it that it was the lady who wrote to you asking for money?"

"It was, but how the devil did you know that?"

"We can leave that lady for the moment. You lunched with her, I suppose?"

"Nothing of the kind. We were not on lunching terms. After seeing her and trying to put some sense into her, I drove back into Portsmouth to lunch at the Crown Hotel. That was where all the trouble started. I was robbed there."

"Robbed?"

"Yes. I parked my overcoat on a peg in the hall and forgot that I had left my note-case in the pocket. I lunched at a table alone. There were half a dozen other people in the dining-room, but I didn't notice any of them particularly. When it came to paying for my lunch I missed my pocket-book and realized that I had left it in my overcoat pocket. I explained to the waiter and went out to fetch it. It had gone: some blighter had pinched it. So there I was without a penny to pay for my lunch and my ticket up to town. I sent for the manager and kicked up a hell of a row. He said that he couldn't be held responsible for things left on the hat-rack. I threatened to sue him—in short, we had quite a nice little row. I suppose that I frightened him and that he telephoned to the Portsmouth police, for in a very few minutes I came into the hall with a telegram to my uncle, and found a queer-looking cove who said he was a detective sent to inquire into what he called the 'alleged theft' of my pocket-book. He had a devil of a lot to say—that they had often had complaints of the kind; that he knew several of the hotel thieves in the town, but that he could not arrest and search them unless the owner of the stolen property was on the spot to identify it. Would I come with him? As there seemed nothing else to do, I went with him."

"You didn't think of asking him to show his warrant-card."

"I didn't know he had such a thing. Well, he took me from pub to pub in the lowest slums in the town, and left me waiting outside while he went in to look for the man he suspected. He didn't stay long in some of them—just looked in and came out again shaking his head; but in some of them he kept me hanging about for a good half-hour."

"Why?"

"Oh, he said that he'd found suspicious characters there and had been interrogating them about their movements."

"You really thought that he was a detective?"

"I was a little doubtful at one point when he had kept me hanging about for half an hour, but when I hinted my suspicions to him he turned nasty and said that I was hindering him in his duty. At the very next pub he arrested a man and came out with him in handcuffs. He said that it wasn't my man, but a man the police had been looking for for a long time. The man was inclined to be violent and I helped to hold him. Then Flaxton—that was the name the detective gave me—asked me to wait while he took him down to police headquarters. He was gone about ten minutes, and he told me when he came back that he had been commended by the chief and that the man had been lodged in a police cell."

"What time was that?"

"Oh, it was getting dark and I was fed-up. I said that I would go back to the ship and see whether I could borrow the money to pay my fare to London as I must get there that evening. You see, my uncle had made a point of that in his letter, and gave me a very good reason for it. Flaxton said, 'If only I'd known that you wanted to get to London I'd have run you up there in the police car. I'll do it now if you'll wait while I bring it round.' He came round with quite a nice Austin and I got in. It was quite dark then, but the headlights were good and he said he knew the road all right. He drove as if the devil was after him. I couldn't see the speedometer in the dark, but it seemed to me that we went as fast through the villages and towns as on the open road. Twice we stopped to take in petrol. He kept assuring me that we should get to London in good time and that he could trust the car. When we were on a stretch of lonely road, all of a sudden the engine conked out. 'Damn!' he said, 'that's the second time she's done that,' and he got down and opened the bonnet. I couldn't see what he was doing, but he asked me to switch on and tread on the self-starter. It was no good: the engine wouldn't start. 'Look here,' he said; 'there's a garage not very far ahead. You stay by the car and I'll walk on to it and bring back a mechanic with me. He'll soon put her right.'"

"What time was it when you broke down?"

"Between nine and ten o'clock. I stuck by the car for hours waiting for him, but he didn't come: at last I got into the back seat and went to sleep, leaving the small lights on. I don't know how long I slept. I woke up with a light in my eyes: a policeman was pulling at my leg. 'Here, wake up,' he shouted at me. 'What are you doing with this car?' I told him what had happened. 'D'you hear that?' he called out to his mate who was sitting on a motorcycle combination. 'The bloke says he's on the way from Portsmouth to London with a detective—not bad for a bloke who's in Somersetshire in a stolen car. He might have told us a better one.' 'What do you mean by saying it's a stolen car?' I said. 'The car belongs to the Portsmouth police.'

"They burst out laughing at that, and said that they had had the number by telephone; that the car was stolen, and that I was wanted for driving at high speed through some tin-pot little town and neglecting to stop when the man on point duty blew his whistle; that I was to come along with them, and the less I said the better. The blighter on the motor-cycle got into the driving-seat and tried to start the car, but the engine wouldn't budge. He got down and began to fool about under the bonnet by the light of the other man's electric torch. They mumbled together in an undertone and then the first man called to me, 'Here, young feller-me-lad, we've had enough of this fooling. You've got the carbon out of the dynamo in your pocket, and you've got to hand it over quick.' I told him that I didn't know what he was talking about. 'Better search him,' said the other man. Then they began pulling me out of the car and I lost my temper. It was a silly thing to do."

"Why, what did you do?"

"Hit one of them a crack on the jaw, and then the fun began. I got a crack on the head from a truncheon and the next thing I knew was that I was handcuffed and lying on the grass by the roadside. One of them went off on the motor-cycle and the other stayed with me. He was inclined to be chatty, but I wasn't taking any. He said, 'When we get you to the station take a tip from me and drop that naval officer stuff of yours. It won't go down with the old man, and when they take your fingerprints and find a list of convictions against you as long as my arm, why—you'll look rather foolish.' In about twenty minutes the other man came back in a car. He pulled a new carbon out of his pocket, shoved it into the dynamo of my car and started her up. By that time it was daylight. They drove for miles and fetched up at a potty little police station in some one-horse town, and fetched a little tin god out of bed to deal with me—a superintendent they called him. The blighter was only half awake and had forgotten to shave the red moss off his chin. They took off the handcuffs and fetched a lot of things out of a cupboard—printing-ink and things—and took my fingerprints. Then the big chief sat down and cleared his throat. 'I am going to charge you,' he said, ' and I must caution you that you are not obliged to say anything, but that anything you say will be taken down in writing and may be used against you at your trial. You are charged with stealing a motor-car (he gave me the number) and with assaulting a police officer in the execution of his duty. Do you wish to say anything?' I said, 'Not until you give me something to eat and drink. Then I shall have a lot to say.' That seemed to put the blighter's back up, but he sent one of his men round the corner for tea and bread and butter and I got outside of them in record time, I can tell you. They watched me do it, and when I'd done I let them have it—told them that I was a naval officer and all the rest of it—told them about the detective who'd left me planted in the car, which he said was a police car from Portsmouth, and that he was driving me up to London in it. They wrote it all down, read it over to me and told me to sign it. Then the big chief with stubble on his chin went to the telephone in another room. I heard part of what he said, but not all. He came back with a grin on his face and said that I'd have to appear before the local bench, and I could tell the beaks the same fairy-story that I'd put in my statement. Did I want a lawyer?

"'Of course I do, if you'll pay for him,' I said. 'I don't suppose he'll work for nothing and I haven't any money.'

"At that he grinned again, but when I asked him to telephone to my captain he wilted a bit and went off to the telephone again. I don't know what happened because they shoved me into a cell and left me there."

"Didn't they bring you before a magistrate?"

"I was coming to that. At eleven o'clock they unlocked me and took me across the street to a room they called the court-house—just a bare room with a desk and a barrier before it. A few loafers followed us into it. The big chief from over the way, all shaved and spruce, yelled 'Silence in Court!' and a benevolent old boy in side-whiskers and spectacles waddled in and took his seat at the desk. 'What's the case, superintendent?'

"'Stealing a motor-car and assaulting the police, y'Washup.' Then he called Daniel Scoop, and the blighter who'd bruised my fist with the point of his lantern jaw took the oath and let himself go.

"'Is anything known about this young man?' asked the beak.

"'He says he's a naval officer, y'Washup. I've 'phoned the Portsmouth police and they're sending up an officer from the *Dauntless* to identify him. I ask you to remand him.'

"So back I went to the cells. They kept me locked up there all yesterday and last night with a plank bed to lie down on. I'll bet you've never been locked up, inspector, so you don't know what it's like, but I can tell you that it's hell. When I got hungry I banged on the door and a policeman put his head in and told me that if I didn't shut up there'd be another charge against me for disturbing the quiet of the cells. I told him that I should go on knocking until I got something to eat. He said, 'That's not the way to get it,' but it was, because he brought me in a plate of cold beef, all cut up into mouthfuls, and when I asked for a knife and fork he said that they weren't allowed—I must eat with my fingers or the best way I could. 'As a remand prisoner,' he said, 'you are entitled to send out for your meals if you pay for them, but as you say that you haven't any money, this is the best I can do for you.' I scarcely slept a wink all last night, and it wasn't until eleven o'clock this morning that they told me that someone had come to see me. I was taken to the superintendent's room and there was my shipmate, Meredith. All he would do was to roar with laughter until I gave him a shove to remind him where we were. Then he identified me all right and told the superintendent that he'd made a big mistake and wouldn't hear the end of it when the Admiralty got to know of it. He said he'd been instructed by the captain to apply for bail. The superintendent bloke looked foolish and went off to his telephone again. When he came back we had both to sign papers letting me out for a week, and I caught the next train to town. Meredith told me that he was the only officer left in the ship when the police came on board yesterday afternoon, and of course he couldn't leave her. He had had a hell of a job to find the captain on the telephone and getting another officer to relieve him. That was the reason for the delay. Now perhaps you'll let me see my uncle."

Foster became serious. "I told you that there had been a burglary here, Mr. Eccles. I must now tell you that it was more than a burglary. There has been a murder."

"Good God! Do you mean my uncle?"

"No, your uncle is upstairs. It was his servant."

Richardson was watching the young man closely and saw him go white.

"Not poor old Helen? How awful!"

"Apparently the poor woman was shot by the man who got in at that window."

"The burglar? My God! I hope you will catch him. If I can do anything to help...Have you any clue?"

"In the shrubbery outside we have found this pocket-book."

"Let me look at it. Why, it's mine: it's the pocket-book that was pinched from me in the hotel at Portsmouth where I lunched!"

Richardson, watching him, felt that the most accomplished actor could never have produced the effect of blank astonishment in his face and manner.

"Yes," he added in an excited tone; "it *is* mine. Look, here are my cards: here's my uncle's letter!" He fumbled in the pocket of the note-case. "The blighter who pinched this was careful to take every penny out of it."

"How much money had you?"

"I cashed a cheque for twenty pounds before I left the ship, but I paid my mess-bill out of it. I suppose I had sixteen or seventeen pounds left and the blighter's pinched it all."

"Were there any Bank of England notes?"

"No, it was all in Treasury notes. But how did my pocket-book get here?"

"If we had the correct answer to that question," remarked Foster dryly, "we should soon know who killed that poor woman. Now I should like to have a description of the man who said he was a detective."

"Flaxton? Oh, he was an inch or two shorter than you and broader. He had a biggish nose and rather pale, shifty-looking blue eyes—you know the kind I mean—just narrow slits. He was clean-shaved except for a light-coloured clipped moustache. His hair was sandy."

"How was he dressed?"

"In a suit of reach-me-downs of a rather flashy check pattern. He was wearing a rather shabby bowler hat with a flat brim."

"Good. Well, now, Mr. Eccles, if you like to go upstairs you'll find your uncle, and in twenty minutes or so your statement will be ready for your signature."

Foster watched his retreating figure as he went upstairs two steps at a time. "Get on with that statement as quick as you can, Richardson; we've a lot before us. All this yarn about the Somerset County Constabulary will have to be checked. I'm going upstairs to see how Mr. MacDougal is taking this story of his."

He found the two closeted in the library: the uncle broken under the strain of the double disaster; the nephew trying to put before him the less gloomy side of the family tragedy. "After all, Uncle Jim, it might have been worse. The blighter might have shot you instead of poor old Helen," he was saying when Foster made his appearance. "Look here, inspector, you can help us. I've been telling my uncle that he must engage another servant at once. Can you tell us where there's a good servants' registry?"

"Not off-hand, Mr. Eccles, but if you telephone to the Hampstead Police Station and explain who you are, they'll tell you. You can mention my name—Superintendent Foster—if you like."

"You won't leave me, Ronny," said MacDougal.

"Not for long, but remember, I've got to get a lawyer to conduct my case when it comes on next week. I'm on bail. I know of a chap named Meredith—the brother of my shipmate who bailed me out. He gave me a chit to him. I'll go and hunt him up this evening and listen to his words of wisdom. If you don't mind I'll go down and telephone for the address of that servants' registry."

"I've one question to ask you, Mr. MacDougal, while your nephew is out of the room," said Foster. "Is he the kind of young man who runs into debt?

"Not more than other young men of his age, I think. I make him a small allowance over and above his naval pay, and it is very seldom that he comes to me for more. When he does I always give it to him."

"Do you know whether he has any entanglements with young women?"

"Not that I have heard of. Why do you ask me that? Has he said anything to you about it?"

"Only because if he had it would account for the scrape he seemed to have got into in Portsmouth."

Richardson knocked at the door and said that the statement was ready for signature. Foster accompanied him downstairs. Ronald Eccles was in the act of disconnecting the telephone, after having come to a satisfactory arrangement with the registry office. He went down with them to the kitchen where the statement was read over to him.

"Have you anything to add to it?" asked Foster.

"Not that I can think of. I'm ready to sign it."

When the two police officers were in the street on their way to the Tube station, Foster asked Richardson what he thought of the statement.

"It sounded a bit thin, sir, but I think we shall find that it was correct."

"You think so? If you're right it means that we're up against a gang. First the thief in the hotel who stole his pocket-book; then a car thief who posed as a detective; and then the man he arrested in the public-house. It means that they read the uncle's letter in the pocket-book and came straight off here to steal the money and plant the pocket-book where Mr. Symington found it in order to throw suspicion on the nephew. Such things have happened, we know, but they are so rare that for me it is easier to believe that that young man was lying. Remember, he wouldn't give me the name and address of the young woman he said he went to see. A man who has something to hide is generally unscrupulous about lying. We shall see what the Somerset police say about his statement."

Chapter Four

THERE WERE two good reasons why Dick Meredith seldom used the lift to his flat on the fourth floor: he had a strong dislike for the pert, red-haired lift-boy, and in running upstairs there was always a sporting chance of meeting the girl who lived in the flat above him—in an eyrie to which the lift did not go. Artfully he had wormed her name out of the hall porter—Miss Patricia Carey—but that was all that the porter knew about her. He himself knew even less, for an occasional meeting on the stairs, when he stood aside to let the vision pass, can scarcely be counted as acquaintance.

Dick Meredith took his practice at the Bar seriously. He knew the story which Lord Chancellor Cairns used to tell about himself—how he owed his start to sticking to his chambers when every other barrister on his staircase had gone to Epsom on Derby Day, and the halting footsteps of a solicitor's clerk sounded on the stairs; how, after trying door after door, they had stopped on his landing, and the knuckles of a solicitor's clerk, carrying an urgent brief marked £5 5s., had summoned him to the door—a brief which was the foundation of his fortunes. No solicitor's clerk had yet blundered into Dick Meredith's chambers with a brief intended for another counsel, but he had appeared before a Judge in Chambers, shaking at the knees, and he went on circuit religiously and had had his modest share of dock briefs, even succeeding by a stroke of luck in getting a Yorkshire jury to find a persistent housebreaker "not guilty."

On a memorable afternoon he was plodding up the fourth flight to his flat when he heard the rush of flying feet on the stairs above him. He drew aside to allow room for the headlong descent. It was the girl whose acquaintance he so ardently desired to make.

"Come quick!" she panted. "James is on the fire." She tore upstairs with Dick at her heels.

"Is James your little brother?"

She did not hear the question. They had reached the top landing; a door stood open. "Quick!" she cried as she dashed in. "Oh, you're safe, you brute!"

It was no way to speak even to a younger and very trying brother. Dick looked round the tiny sitting-room. A dull fire was burning in the grate; a yellow-fronted Amazon parrot was perched on the back of a chair; there was a strong smell of burnt feathers.

The girl was profuse in apology. "I'm so sorry to have brought you up all this way for nothing, but when I ran downstairs for help that brute James flew from his cage on to the fire and was sitting on it."

"I've read somewhere that the cock parrot takes his turn at sitting on the eggs. He may be colour-blind. Those little lumps of coal are about the size of parrot's eggs. Never mind, I'm grateful to James for the introduction. My name is Meredith. James speaks so indistinctly that I didn't catch yours."

"Mine is Patricia Carey, but I don't want you to think that that horrid bird is mine: he belongs to the old gentleman I work for. I ought not to be calling him names. I owe him a month's leave on full pay."

"Absolutely," remarked the parrot with sepulchral decision.

Dick Meredith started and looked round for the speaker. The girl laughed merrily.

"James gave you a start. 'Absolutely' is Mr. Vance's favourite affirmative and James has caught it from him."

"How did he get you a month's leave on full pay?"

"The condition attached to my leave was that I should have to give a home to that bird while Mr. Vance was going round foreign prisons—they call him the 'Second John Howard,' you know—and he's let me down on the very first day. Mr. Vance told me that if I let him sit on the top of his cage in the daytime he could be trusted to behave himself, and the first thing he did when I let him out just now was to fly straight on to the fire and sit on the coals as if he meant to hatch them."

"Well, he had the sense to get off in time. You're a stout fellow, James."

The bird ruffled his neck and bowed his head to be stroked.

"He seems to have taken a fancy to you. He hates me."

"Absolutely," remarked James with marked distinctness.

"Does he talk much?" asked Dick, caressing him.

"He's a good weather prophet. He's much more reliable than the B.B.C. When it's going to rain he goes down to the bottom of his cage and chatters gibberish. I suppose—" She hesitated.

"You were going to say?"

The girl laughed nervously. "Oh, nothing. I nearly made a silly suggestion—that as he's taken to you so quickly—well—that you might like to have him in your flat for a few days."

"I should love to, but it's a big responsibility. Still—if you would look in from time to time to see that he's all right—"

"Well—I *was* going down to my people in the country for a few days if I hadn't been saddled with James—" She had the grace to blush at the audacity of her manoeuvre.

"I'll take charge of him with pleasure if you'll give me his diet chart. I suppose that it's rather complicated."

"Not at all. The greedy little brute eats anything. I was just going to give him buttered toast when he chose to go and sit on the fire." She caught Dick's eye roving to the tea-table. "You'll have some tea, won't you?"

During the next half-hour their acquaintance ripened. They found themselves talking as if they had known one another for years. Dick learned that she was the daughter of a country parson in Sussex, and that, having her own living to make, she had been trained as a secretary; that through the influence of one of her father's friends she had been lucky enough to get a job as private secretary to the famous James Vance.

Observing the blank look in her visitor's face she exclaimed in shocked surprise, "You've never heard of him?"

"Never."

"But surely you've heard of Vance's Rejuvenator, the patent medicine that you see advertised everywhere."

"No, I never take patent medicines."

"Nor do I, but evidently quite a lot of people do: otherwise Mr. Vance wouldn't have made his millions. Surely you know those short stories in the magazines which are quite interesting until you are brought up quite suddenly by something like this—'that's why I took to Vance's Rejuvenator.'"

"I never read magazines now that they've taken to the American trick of breaking off at the exciting point and telling you to hunt for the rest on page 937."

"Yes, but I should have thought you would have heard of Mr. Vance's activities in other directions. He's a Manchester man, and his present craze is prison reform. As far as I can make out he would like to convert prisons into rest-houses run on the lines of Sunday schools."

"I didn't know that there were such people nowadays. How is he setting about it?"

"That's the trouble. Providence has denied to Mr. Vance one gift—the gift of public speaking—and for the matter of that, the gift of writing grammatical English. I have to do that for him. The letters he dictates are simply awful, but luckily he never suspects that I've written all he wanted to say in half the length and in passable English."

"You don't do his public speaking for him?"

Patricia laughed merrily. "No, I haven't got as far as that yet. He subsidizes young men to do it for him: he has a small army of them."

"Do they believe in him?"

"They say they do; one or two of them certainly do—Mr. Ralph Lewis, for instance. You've heard of him?"

"I've seen his name in the papers, but I'm afraid I've never troubled to read his speeches. Don't the Liberal papers call him 'the coming man'?"

"I believe they're right. I've heard him speak. He carries you right off your feet. You really ought to go and hear him."

"Perhaps I will—some day."

His indifference pricked her like a goad. "I suppose that when *you* go out in the evening you waste your time at some musical comedy, but I promise you that if once you hear Ralph Lewis he'll carry you away as he did me."

"I hate political speeches and the men who make them. What is the special point about this one?"

"Well, to begin with he's very good-looking and he has a wonderful voice. I've seen his audience in tears, and the tears running down his own cheeks. One night there was a little knot of interrupters, and people were calling to the chairman to have them put out, but Mr. Lewis just raised his hand and turned his face to the part of the hall where they were. They told me afterwards that before he had finished they were crying too."

"What does he say?"

"Oh, one can't remember what he says. I suppose it's the way he says it."

"I'll go and hear him if you'll take me, but now you must be longing to do your packing. James and I will leave you to it. But you must give me your address in case he seems to be sickening for psittacosis."

With her card in his pocket, Dick Meredith approached James, who allowed himself to be immured in his cage with the greatest amiability, and was carried down to the floor below.

As Dick was fumbling with his latch-key, the lift shot up to his floor-level: the gate clanged back and the figure of his pet aversion, red-haired Albert, who looked as if he had been poured into his suit of buttons, strutted out full of importance, with a letter and a visiting-card between finger and thumb. Dick set down the cage to receive them.

"Gentleman waiting downstairs to see you," said Albert.

"Absolutely," remarked the parrot, who seemed to have a warm feeling for the young of the human species.

While Dick was reading his letter Albert improved the occasion by whistling a lively air and ejaculating "Pretty Polly," greeting each "Absolutely" with a scream of ribald laughter. "Going to take charge of Miss Carey's parrot?" he asked.

"Bring the gentleman up," said Dick, without deigning to reply to the question. The name on the card conveyed nothing to Dick, but the letter was addressed in the handwriting of his sailor brother, whose ship, as he knew, had just berthed in Portsmouth for a refit.

"DEAR DICK," he wrote, "This is to introduce my shipmate Eccles, who's been having words with the police. I told him that you were the man to save him from the gallows, or if that's not in your line you would pass him on to the right bloke.

"Yours,

"BIM."

Ronald Eccles used the lift and was at the door within three minutes. Having conceived all lawyers to be austere-looking persons who cultivated side-whiskers and bald heads, he seemed relieved to find in Dick a man of his own age to whom he could talk freely. After the usual greetings Dick opened the business.

"My brother tells me that you've had trouble with the police? A motoring offence, I suppose."

"It's worse than that. I'm on remand for stealing a car and assaulting a constable, and I want some-body to take up my case."

Dick looked at him quizzically and decided in his own mind that he did not look the sort of man who would spend his first night ashore by painting the town red. "I think that you had better tell me the whole story before I can advise you what to do."

He listened without interrupting his visitor except to interject a question here and there, and when Eccles came to the discovery by the police of his stolen pocket-book in the garden of his uncle's house in London, and of the murder and the burglary, he began to show a quickened interest.

"Can you give me a description of the man who took you round the public-houses, pretending to be a detective?"

"He was decently dressed and about the same height as I am. He wore a bowler hat, a bit worse for wear; he had a thin face and rather cunning little eyes."

"Did you take him for a detective as soon as you saw him?"

"Well—no. I couldn't place the blighter at first. I thought he might be one of these reporter chaps who wanted to pump me about our cruise for the local rag, but when he told me that he was a detective I was fool enough to believe him."

"Did the man he arrested in the public-house behave as a criminal would if a detective pounced on him suddenly?"

"He kept saying, 'You've made a mistake, Guv'nor. Beale's not my name,' and when my man stuck to it that it was, he turned nasty and tried to wriggle himself free until I got hold of his other arm. Then he said, 'All right, Guv'nor, I'll go quiet, but leave go of my arm: you're hurting me.'"

"How was he dressed?"

"Like a dock labourer, I should say. I remember that his clothes didn't seem to fit him and that he'd a dirty muffler round his neck instead of a collar. But I'd know him again if I saw him. I'd know them both. There's another thing about Flaxton, the detective, which I suppose you ought to know. He had a folded newspaper sticking out of his left pocket: it fell out on the seat when he was driving and he left it behind when he went off. It was a *Mercury*, and one of the paragraphs was heavily marked in blue pencil—something about a political meeting in Cardiff addressed by a political bloke named Ralph Lewis."

"Have you still got the paper?" asked Dick, trying to disguise his interest.

"Yes, here it is."

Dick Meredith read the paragraph, headlines and all. It described the meeting and gave a brief resume of Lewis's speech, referring to the speaker as a young Liberal of whom more was likely to be heard in the near future. "May I keep this paper?" he asked.

"Certainly. Keep it as long as you like. I don't want it back."

"You haven't shown it to the police?"

"Good Lord, no! I've had enough of the police to last me for the rest of my natural life."

"I think they ought to be told, but you can leave that to me, if you like. Now, on the face of your story, three men were members of the same gang—the man who pinched your pocket-book in the hotel, the sham detective, and the man he pretended to arrest. Apparently you can identify two of them. I suppose that you don't care to tell me how you spent the morning between the time you left the ship and the time you sat down to lunch?"

"Oh, that has nothing whatever to do with the case."

"Very well. Now the part of the business that really presses is to clear you of the charges in Somersetshire on which you are remanded. For that you must employ a solicitor, and I can give you the name and address of the very man..."

Eccles' face fell. "I hoped that you would undertake the case yourself."

"I'm a barrister, not a solicitor, and a barrister can't undertake a case except on instructions from a solicitor."

"But if I tell the solicitor that I'd rather have you?

"Ah, then it would rest with him, but to employ counsel to represent you in what is now a preliminary hearing in a police court would double your costs."

"Oh, blow the expense! My uncle told me to get the best man whatever it cost."

"Then hold on while I scribble a note to the solicitor. You'll find a cigarette-box at your elbow and whisky and a siphon on that sideboard. Help yourself while I'm writing."

The silence was broken only by the fizz of the siphon as it squirted a few thimblefulls into the glass, for Eccles was a young man who did not believe in drowning good liquor. He was feeling more at peace with the world now that he was in the hands of this sensible and competent young man who knew what to do and how to do it. Before he had had time to empty his glass his host rose from his writing-table.

"Here's the note. You'll find the name in the Law List and the Telephone Directory. In your place I should ring him up, tell him who you are, and say that you have a note from me and you would like to make an appointment for to-morrow morning. Stop—I forgot that probably you haven't a club in London. I'll ring him up for you."

Dick went to his telephone, and Ronald Eccles listened to one half of the conversation. "Meredith speaking—yes—Dick Meredith. Are you full up for to-morrow morning?—No, nothing of the kind. I've a naval officer here—a friend of my brother—who wants to consult you. He's in trouble with the Somerset Constabulary. It seems from what he's told me to be an interesting case—one after your own heart...at what time?... ten o'clock? Good, he'll be there."

As soon as Meredith was alone he picked up the newspaper again, reflecting that it was a remarkable coincidence that he had twice encountered the name of Ralph Lewis on the same afternoon, and that a man denounced to him as a car-thief should have been carrying a newspaper with a paragraph about Lewis marked in blue.

"Curious, isn't it, James?"

"Absolutely," agreed the parrot.

James had taken kindly to his new quarters, and for the first eighteen hours all went well. He rattled at his cage door, demanding liberty; climbed to the roof of his prison and surveyed the world with one yellow eye; bowed his green head for caresses, and seemed to take no note of the open window or of the sunshine streaming through it. Dick wished that his temporary mistress had looked in on her way downstairs to see what an admirable caretaker he was, but he had heard her pass his door with her suit-case early that morning. And then, as he turned away from the cage, came the catastrophe. His foot caught the leg of the stool on which the cage was standing. Feeling the foundations of his solid world rocking beneath him, James might have been forgiven for what he did. With a whir of his green wings he shot across the room and out through the open window into the vast spaces of London.

Dick ran to the window in the vain hope that he would be able to take the bearings of James's flight, but he was out of sight. Surely, thought Dick, he must have made for one of the parks: row upon row of chimney-pots would have little attraction for a bird reared in a Brazilian forest. The first obvious step was to advertise; the second to invoke the help of the Metropolitan Police. He rang up the Advertisement manager of the *Daily Mail* and dictated an advertisement offering a generous reward to James's finder, dismissing the thought that the hall-porter downstairs would be beset next day by persons of both sexes with Amazon parrots for whom they had failed to find a market. Then he betook himself to the police station to take counsel with the sergeant in charge.

The station sergeant listened to his story with cleverly simulated sympathy. "You say that the bird took to flight this morning, sir."

"Yes, not half an hour ago."

"Then, sir, he's pretty sure to be in one of the squares, or in Chelsea Hospital Gardens, or in Hyde Park. Quite a number of parrots are lost in London, but I'm afraid that the owners don't very often get them back. I remember one that was loose in St. James's Park for an entire summer and autumn. It used to come down to feed with the ducks. I suppose the cold weather in the winter killed the poor thing, but the owner never got him back though he offered a good reward for him."

Dick went on to his club to ask for letters. He was turning away from the porter's box in deep dejection when a hand tapped him on the shoulder. He turned to find his Canadian friend, Jim Milsom, a cheerful, irresponsible young man reputed to be the heir to a millionaire uncle.

He scrutinized Dick's face gravely. "What's the matter, old man? Have you been backing a loser, or having a dust-up with a judge?"

"Neither. I'm all right."

"Bunk! Something's been biting you. Where's the merry smile? Come into the card-room and unburden your soul. Consultations free from two to four."

Dick allowed himself to be led. Milsom rang for drinks.

"Now that we're alone, out with it. These walls have no ears."

"What would you do if someone left you in charge of a parrot and you lost it?"

"I shouldn't make a song about that. I'd go down to the docks and buy its double."

"And lie about it?"

"A lie is a very present help in trouble. If the lie would bring happiness to a stricken home it will bring its reward. But maiden aunts who dote on parrots deserve all that's coming to them."

"The owner of this bird isn't a maiden aunt, and she hated it," said Dick warmly.

"Well, then, she'll be grateful to you."

"You don't understand. I'd better tell you the whole story."

His irrepressible friend heard him out and began to chuckle.

"This is a job for an expert, old man. You'll have to leave it to me. You say he's a yellow-fronted Amazon. I know the brutes well. They're dressed in the worst possible taste—bilious green, with touches of coral pink in the wrong places, and a thoroughly vicious yellow eye. There are dozens of them down at the docks, as like one another as golf-balls."

"It's no good, my dear fellow. You couldn't find one that croaks 'Absolutely' with appalling distinctness. Unless your bird did that the fraud would be detected at once."

"Lord! That's nothing. All you have to do is to stick my bird in a dark boot-cupboard for forty-eight hours and repeat the word to him in a parrot-sort-of-voice for three hours a day without stopping, and then you take him in to the lady, and she says, 'Is this really my bird?' and he says, 'Absolutely,' and she falls into your arms crying, 'My preserver,' and the scene fades out to slow music."

"Dash it! Her flat's just overhead. If she heard me chanting 'Absolutely' for hours on end she'd ring up for the looney squad and get me put away."

"Then I'll do the training. The man overhead in my flat is a futurist painter and he's been certifiable for months past. Now, Dick, I've listened to your tale of woe and I'll have you listen to mine, and give me a little of the professional advice for which you are so justly famous."

"I'll listen to you as long as you like if you'll just give me time to send a telegram. Sit tight while I take it down to the porter."

He ran downstairs, and after a brief search in his pocket-book for Patricia's address and a telegraph form, handed the following message to the porter:

"MISS PATRICIA CAREY, VICARAGE, WENDLESHAM.

James lost. Very sorry.—MEREDITH."

Chapter Five

"Now I'm ready to hear the worst," said Dick, flinging himself into a chair after dispatching his telegram.

"Well—as I've told you before, when I've nothing better to do, I like to slip down to the London docks. They've a sort of fascination for me."

"Take care, old man; I've heard that it grows upon a man like drink. What's the attraction?"

"Oh, the ships and the men who sail in them, I suppose. Sometimes I run across old friends, and there are always the bird and animal merchants. I was looking into my pet bird-fancier—an old ruffian who buys birds from the sailors—or rather, did buy them before the doctors who didn't like parrots invented the disease of psittacosis to account for diseases they couldn't cure. While I was talking to him, a guy poked me in the back. I swung round on him and I'm damned if it wasn't Harding Moore—a guy we used to call 'Poker' Moore because of his poker dial when he used to play the game he lived on. I must have told you about him?"

"Have you?" said Dick absently. "I don't remember it."

"Well, listen. Poker Moore has about as much expression in his face as a cow looking at a passing train: he has eyes like a boiled cod, and a nose and mouth to match. I'd dare you to guess what he's thinking about. 'What ho, Poker,' I said. 'What brings you over?' 'Never mind what brought me over,' he said, 'but if you want to know, I'll tell you. I've an account to square.'"

"An account to square?"

"That's what he said, and when a man like Poker says that, you've got to sit up and take notice, because he means what he says. He went on to tell me that the guy he was looking for was a young Welshman named Owen Jones."

Dick Meredith permitted himself to yawn. He had graver things to think about than the ups and downs of professional card-players.

"Most Welshmen are named Owen Jones, aren't they?"

"That's what I said. I asked him how he was going to find him. 'I've found him already, my boy,' he said. 'Look at this.' He pulled out of his pocket a poster of a meeting at the Albert Hall and pointed to a portrait on it. 'That's my man,' he said. It was a picture of the principal speaker at the meeting—a guy called Ralph Lewis."

If Dick had been inattentive up to this point, he made up for it now. "How did your friend think that Owen Jones could be Ralph Lewis when the name was staring him in the face?"

"That's exactly what I said to him, but I never got the mystery cleared up, because at that moment one of his pals barged in and they went off together. Before he went Poker gave me his address—Suffolk Hotel, Bloomsbury—and I gave him mine. He said that he would come round and dine with me to tell me the rest of his story, but he never came. I rang up the Suffolk Hotel and they told me that he had gone away without his luggage and without paying his bill—they didn't know where. That was six days ago and I've never seen or heard of him since."

"Perhaps he went off somewhere with his friend. In any case, he's not in the least likely to find the man he's looking for."

"So anyone might say if he didn't know Poker Moore, but when Poker's on the job, you could safely back him against any ferret. Besides, he thinks that he's run the man to ground already."

"You mean Ralph Lewis? He can take care of himself. He hasn't got a past."

"Hasn't he? Why, everybody's got a past. You might not think it, but I have a sultry past. I once kidnapped a child."

"Oh, do be serious."

"It's a fact. It was only my appealing eyes that saved me from prosecution and a long term in a penitentiary. But never mind about me. This guy, Harding Moore, means to attend that meeting in the Albert Hall and lay the speaker out."

"Give him a thrashing, you mean?"

"If he stopped at beating him up, I wouldn't raise a finger to stop him. The young politician who's set on making a living out of the politics business is asking for it, but Poker Moore, if I know the guy, won't stop at beating an enemy up. He's got a gun. Now, I don't want to see poor old Poker in the condemned cell, but that's where he's likely to be if we don't get busy. Suppose he bores a hole in the wrong guy?"

"If he's going on a portrait on a poster, he will. Would you mind telling me where I come in?"

"As a man of law to keep me straight. I'd rather take your advice than any solicitor's. You know what a solicitor would do— pull a long face and advise me to go to Scotland Yard, and then some heavy-footed sleuth would be put on the heels of Poker, and he'd turn on the blighter and cop him one on the jaw, and I'd have to go down and bail him out. No, Dick, old man, your advice is good enough for me."

"I'm not sure that I shouldn't give you the same advice—to go to Scotland Yard. Does it matter very much to you if your friend, Moore, does assault Ralph Lewis?"

Jim Milsom's eye roved meditatively over the past. "Poker Moore did me a big service at the risk of his life years ago, and I shouldn't like him to think that there was a streak of yellow in me."

"I understand. Give me to-day to think it over, and come and see me to-morrow."

The more Dick thought over what he had been told, the less he liked it. If this professional gambler had mistaken Ralph Lewis for another man, as it was evident that he had, and in that belief assaulted, and, in Jim Milsom's expressive phrase, "beat him up," Lewis would become a greater hero than before to his flapper band of admirers. Ought he, Dick Meredith, to waste an evening listening to this rising political luminary? His blood ran cold at the very thought of it. True, he had half-promised Patricia that he would, but that was in those happier days when she trusted him—before that little demon, James, took to wing, carrying her trust with him.

He lunched at the Temple and listened to the gossip of his fellow-lunchers. Then back in his chambers again, he tried to distract his mind by work, but at five o'clock he took the Underground to Sloane Square and went home.

The loathly Albert met him on the doorstep to impart information. "Miss Carey's back from the country. She's in a terrible way about her parrot you lost."

Dick could have relieved his feelings by kicking him behind as he retreated, but he forbore. If Patricia was upstairs, he must go and make his peace with her if he could. Rejecting Albert's offer of the lift, he toiled up to the fifth floor and tapped at Patricia's door. She found a figure of contrition standing on the doormat. "I'm awfully sorry," it began.

"James *must* be found," she said firmly, feeling that with people lacking in the sense of responsibility firmness was the only possible attitude.

"I've done everything I could think of—advertised a big reward and applied to the police."

"How did it happen?"

"May I come in and explain?" He felt that her manner as a hostess lacked something of the sense of welcome. "I don't know what possessed that bird. He seemed to have quite taken to me—let me scratch his head, showed a strong partiality for buttered toast at breakfast-time, and behaved as if the butter wouldn't melt in his beak. He kept rattling at the cage door, so I let him out—"

"And left the window open? I might have known it."

"Certainly the window did happen to be open, but to do the bird justice, I don't believe that he was thinking of the window.

He was quite happy with me. No, it was an accident that made him take to wing. I'll make a clean breast of it. My foot caught against the foot of the stool under his cage—"

"And naturally he took to wing. He's done that before, but though his master may be a prosy old man, he never had the window open when James was out of his cage. It was my fault for leaving him with a stranger."

"Do you think that it's fair to call me a stranger? You might justly call me a fool for not thinking of the window, but not a stranger. After all, we live under the same roof—in fact, I was going to ask you to come out and dine with me to-night—to make plans for getting James back. I feel sure that we shall get him back."

"Thank you, but I couldn't go out and amuse myself while he's lost. You don't seem to realize that if he's not found it will cost me my job."

"But not even John Howard himself could possibly blame *you*, and as for James, he's probably having the time of his life with the other lost parrots in the Park. He'd hate you to mourn."

Dick regretted his flippancy the moment the words had passed his lips. He saw that the girl was facing the crisis in her life and was in no mood for jesting. Indeed, he could see that she was very near to tears. He rose awkwardly. "I see that you don't believe that I'm doing all I can—that I don't realize all it means to you, so I'll take myself off. The moment I hear anything of James I'll ring you up. When we've got him back, as I'm sure we shall, we'll laugh over the bad time we're both going through."

Patricia relented. "Won't you sit down, Mr. Meredith? I don't want you to think me ungrateful when you were so good in making it possible for me to go home and see my people. If I seemed ungrateful it was only because your telegram was a great shock to me. Tell me what you are doing, and let us talk over what we can do next."

They sat talking for nearly half an hour—not exclusively about the missing bird. "I hear that your friend, Ralph Lewis, is to speak at the Albert Hall in a few days, and that the meeting is being advertised on posters. Are you going to hear him?"

"I ought to if I'm in London. Mr. Vance is sure to ask me how he was received."

"Do you think I might come with you? I should like to hear him," added Dick mendaciously.

"Very well. We'll go together, if you like...I'll watch your conversion."

Dick noticed that she blushed with pleasure, but he thought bitterly that it was on account of the speaker, not at the prospect of his company.

"I suppose that Ralph Lewis is a Welshman; it's a Welsh name."

"Yes, he comes from Wales."

"Has he any relations there?"

"I heard someone say that he has a host of them." Having done his best to thaw the ice-barrier that the recreant James had erected between them, Dick returned to his rooms on the floor below and brooded. Jim Milsom's plan of buying another parrot and educating it to ejaculate the word "Absolutely" no longer seemed fantastic. It would have to be done—otherwise the knowledge that he had ruined Patricia's prospects would haunt him through life. James was not her property. Surely she would not judge harshly the fraud of personation. But James's owner! Would he be taken in so easily? The modern John Howard! A philanthropist who thought he had a mission in life! Surely he was just the kind of man who would swallow anything. But if he didn't! If, for example, Jim Milsom's changeling bit him on the finger when he went to scratch his head—if he had learned sailors' profanity on the voyage from Brazil and let forth a string of bad language at a meeting of earnest prison-reformers in the modern John Howard's dining-room, Patricia's fate would be sealed. Either the bird would be detected as a changeling, or she would be accused of teaching him to swear. In either case she would be discharged without a character. She would never confess that she had trusted so precious a bird as James to the care of a comparative stranger, because that in itself would be enough to procure her dismissal.

He was brooding thus when his telephone bell became agitated.

"Is that you, Meredith?" called a voice.

"It is."

"That naval officer of yours, Eccles, turned up this morning. He told me a fantastic sort of story. I suppose that one can believe him?"

"I think so."

"He wants me to brief you to defend him at the adjourned hearing by the Somersetshire Bench. What about it?"

"I'll go if you think it's worth it, but why should he put himself to that expense? You could get a local man to represent him."

"He wouldn't hear of that. Though he was innocent of the charge of car-stealing, he was guilty of hitting a policeman, and he doesn't want the case to get into the papers; otherwise, he says, the Admiralty may chalk him up in his service record as an officer given to brawling with policemen."

"All right, then. I'll go if you'll send me round the brief, and I'll see what I can do to keep the local reporter quiet."

Dick's chief interest in his naval client's case was that paragraph marked in blue in the newspaper left in the stolen car. It was the third time in two days that the name of Ralph Lewis had cropped up, and now he had engaged himself to waste an evening in listening to the young man in the company of someone who was more interested in the young man than he liked. Then what had become of Jim Milsom's friend who was out for Lewis's blood? This thought was uppermost in his mind next morning when three ponderous raps sounded on his door.

"Come in, Milsom. I recognized your manner of announcing yourself. Have you heard anything of your missing friend?"

"Not a word. I tell you, it's a queer business. It isn't a bit like Poker not to drop me a word to say that something had stopped him from coming to dinner, and he's not the man to go off without letting me know. I don't know what to think."

"He may have forgotten your address."

"Damn it! I gave him an addressed envelope and saw him pouch it. And then he went off and left all his luggage behind him in the hotel—didn't even pay his hotel bill before he went. That's not like Poker. He's a careful man in things like that. No, there's something queer."

"Then my advice to you is to inform the people at the Yard, or let me do it. I have to see them on another matter. It's part of their job to protect people when they're in danger."

"All right: go ahead."

"By the way, you never told me whether you bought that parrot."

"Did I not? You'll find him in my flat any time you're passing—that is, if you look into the boot-cupboard for a cage built for a canary-bird. I haven't had time to give him the language-lessons, but he talks. I wouldn't like to pollute your ears with what he says at present. He's been keeping bad company in the fo'castle, but he'll forget it all when he's word-perfect. You said that 'Abso-bally-lutely' was the word I had to teach him?"

"Don't start pulling my leg. You know perfectly well what the word was—'Absolutely.'"

Chapter Six

THE FILE on the Hampstead murder was growing thick: besides Superintendent Foster's report on his investigations up to date, there were reports from the Chief Constables of Portsmouth and Somersetshire, bearing out the statements of Lieutenant Eccles up to a certain point. His arrest in a stolen car at 2 a.m. and his assault on a constable of the County Police, for which offences he had been remanded for eight days, were confirmed by the Chief Constable: the Portsmouth police reported that they had had an interview with the landlord of the Crown Hotel, who remembered that on the date in question a gentleman had complained of having had a pocket-book stolen from his overcoat hanging in the hall; that a visitor had asked for the gentleman a few minutes later and had whispered to him that he was a detective; that the two had gone off together and therefore the landlord had made no report of the incident to the police, because he assumed that the gentleman himself had done so. The report went on to say that no detective on the strength of the Portsmouth police was authorized to interview any person in the Crown Hotel, nor did any officer bring in a prisoner in handcuffs that afternoon.

Foster's report ended with a request for authority to send Sergeant Richardson down to Portsmouth to make inquiries, and it was chiefly on this request that Charles Morden, always a stickler for economy, had summoned Foster to his room. As a barrister of several years' criminal practice at the Bar before he joined the Criminal Investigation Department, Morden was a tower of strength whenever legal questions of procedure were involved. With his pale, short-sighted eyes, which blinked whenever he looked up, his soft voice and his studious air, he would have been easily mistaken for a college don; he was popular with the staff because he sympathized with their difficulties and was more prone to give encouragement that blame, but all knew that when blame was deserved it would be given with no stinting hand.

"I've been reading through these reports, Mr. Foster, and it seems to me that you are up against a gang of three men at least—the man who stole Eccles' pocket-book, the sham detective who stole a car and prevented Eccles from going up to London, and the man he pretended to arrest in that public-house. I see that he gave a fair description of the sham detective."

"He said that he could identify the last two if he saw them."

"I see that you want to send Richardson to Portsmouth, but how will that help? I don't want to incur the expense unless it is likely to lead to something tangible."

"I think that it may, sir. There are several things to clear up. First there is that money-lender whose address is on the letter found in the pocket-book: next I want him to have a talk with the Portsmouth C.I.D. and see whether they can throw any light upon the man who posed as a detective. Probably it's not the first time he's done it. Next, I want him to see the County Constabulary and see what suggestions they can make about the identity of the woman living on a farm near Portsmouth who wrote to Lieutenant Eccles asking for two hundred pounds—the woman he went out to see when he left his ship. You remember, sir, that he refused to give me her name and address."

"Then you haven't yet dismissed Lieutenant Eccles from the case?"

"No, sir. In my opinion it's too soon to do that. The reports from the Provincial Police corroborate only part of his statement, and a man who declines to give a full account of his movements has something to hide. He was in need of money; he knew that there was a large sum in his uncle's house; his pocket-book was picked up on the scene of the crime."

"But a man cannot be in two places at one and the same time—in a police cell in Somersetshire and in his uncle's house on the night of the murder."

"Quite true, sir, but what would prevent him from sending another man up to London to break into the house and to be in that stolen car and assault the police to make his alibi safe?"

"I haven't seen the young man and you have, so I can't pretend to judge, but he must be a very exceptional sort of naval officer if he robbed his uncle and murdered his servant after laying elaborate plans to support his alibi." Morden was dying to ask a direct question, but instinct warned him that it would be wiser to approach it obliquely. "Do you think that Sergeant Richardson is the man for this inquiry in the West of England? How is he shaping in the case?"

"Very well, sir. Of course he's young and his head is a bit too full of the stuff he learned in the detective class."

"In what way?" asked Morden with interest, for he took a particular pride in the instruction given in the detective class.

"Well, he fusses about taking fingerprints and footprints and that kind of thing." Foster smiled reminiscently. "He's a regular walking arsenal of gadgets—white and black powder, plaster of Paris, callipers and the like. I'm sure that if I were to ask him for a crocodile's tooth he'd produce one from that attaché case of his."

"And I see from your report that he can take down statements in shorthand. But for the job you want to give him, Mr. Foster, he ought to be a good judge of character as well. Remember, he's young, and he will have to interview a number of senior officers down there who are sure to be a little on their dignity. We must not run the risk of ruffling it."

"You need not be afraid of that, sir. Richardson has excellent manners with his seniors, and they all seem to like him. He's the sort of young officer who might form a poor opinion of their judgment, but would never let them know it."

Now, thought Morden, is the moment for the question. "What view did he take of Lieutenant Eccles' statement?"

Foster laughed indulgently. "Oh, he swallowed everything he said—swallowed it whole but he's young and impulsive, and I'm sure that he'll grow out of that as his experience increases."

"Very well, you can send him down. I don't want to hamper you, but in these days we must all feel ourselves to be custodians of the public purse. What are you doing about those footprints found in the front garden?"

"I'm going to Redford myself to-morrow afternoon, sir, and I'm taking Richardson's plaster casts with me. I shall get the Redford police to take me out to Jackson's farm and have a look at his boots. If I find a piece missing from the heel-plate of the left boot, as it is in the plaster cast, I shall take a statement from Jackson and get him to account for his second visit to the house that evening. I shall be back this evening in case that I'm wanted, sir."

"Didn't Symington find some footprints in the shrubbery near that pocket-book?"

"Yes, sir, he did, but they weren't good enough to take a plaster cast from. I've had them accurately measured, and if we get further evidence pointing to Lieutenant Eccles, I shall compare his shoes with the measurements."

Richardson took the night train to Portsmouth and slept as well as he could in a crowded third-class compartment. His first visit was to the Crown Hotel very early next morning. He asked the night-porter for facilities for washing and shaving, and learned in the course of conversation that he expected to be relieved by his colleague on the day-shift at 7 a.m. It was the day-porter that Richardson wished to see before seeking an interview with the manager. Breakfast in the Crown Hotel was, in his judgment, quite beyond the purse of a third-class detective-sergeant: breakfast would have to wait.

The night-porter's relief interpreted his hours liberally: he arrived fourteen minutes late, but Richardson guessed correctly that the two men worked on the principle of give-and-take: at any rate, when they met there was no apology. The day-porter went to his desk and Richardson approached him.

"Good morning. I've come down by the night train."

"You want breakfast, sir? I'll ring—"

"No thank you," smiled Richardson, adding mendaciously, "I've had a bite of breakfast. Let me see—I believe that you were porter here when I came down from London six months ago." It was a second deviation from the truth: this was Richardson's first visit to Portsmouth.

"Lord! Sir, I've been here near on three years. You'll excuse me for not recalling your face. We have such a lot of people passing through."

"Of course you have. I should have been very much surprised if you had recognized me." Richardson had returned to the paths of rectitude. "I want to ask you a question or two. I must explain that I'm a detective-sergeant from Scotland Yard."

The porter stiffened. "I'm sorry, sir, but I've already been let down once by a person who said he was a detective, and it turned out afterwards that he wasn't. There was a lot of trouble over it with Mr. Yule, our manager, and he's given strict orders that anyone who calls and says that he's a 'tec is to be taken to him."

Richardson produced his warrant-card. "If you'll kindly cast your eye over that you'll see that you're dealing with the real article. The reason I've come to you first is to get a good description of the man who got you into trouble by saying he was a detective, because we're looking for him now."

"Now you're talking, sir. If I can do anything to get that feller into quod for what he did, why I'm your man. I'd know him again anywhere. He was medium height—about five feet eight, I should say—stockily built—small mouth and clipped moustache—shifty sort of grey eyes—and dressed in a grey cutaway suit and bowler hat. To tell you the honest truth, when he first came in I took him for a commercial, travelling in joolry or tailoring and I wondered why he was coming to us instead of one of them commercial hotels."

"He gave you no name?"

"No, and I didn't ask for one until he said that he wanted to see Lieutenant Eccles; and then he didn't give it because Mr.

Eccles himself chanced to come into the hall at that moment, and I told him that there was a gent asking for him."

"Then you noticed nothing special about him—about his manner, or speech, or way of walking?"

The porter searched his memory for a minute.

"I do remember one thing about him that seemed funny at the time. He spoke like a Londoner; he called himself a detective, as I told you, but his hands were rough-like, with short thick fingers—more like the hands of a man who's had rough work to do day after day."

At this point the porter was called away to do the honours to some new arrivals, but Richardson stood by the desk. He had other things to ask him. When the man returned, he said, "You've given me a pretty good description of that man. I wonder whether you can remember another who was here during the lunch-hour of the same day."

"Oh you mean some thief that the naval officer said had picked his overcoat pocket while he was at lunch in the dining-room. No, I can't for the very good reason that I get a half-hour off for lunch just at that time, and there's nobody left in the hall but a page-boy, who is there to show people into the dining-room and call me if I'm wanted. But do you think that Mr. Eccles really had his pocket-book pinched? I've my doubts about it."

"Why?"

"Well, you see those pegs over there? That's gentlemen hang their overcoats. It's in full view through the glass panels of the dining-room, and if a stranger walked in and went straight to the coats, either the boy or the girl at the desk would think it funny and ask him what he was doing. Of course, if it was someone who'd been lunching in the dining-room it would be different, but I knew them all by sight, or nearly all."

"Nearly all? There were one or two strangers then?"

"Yes, two or three. I didn't take special notice of any of them."

"Where would they hang their coats?"

"On those pegs over there. There's no other place."

"Did you notice whether any of them left the hotel before Lieutenant Eccles?"

"No, I didn't."

Richardson was less successful with Mr. Yule, the hotel manager, than he had a right to expect. He found the gentleman in a little office behind the reception counter, and introduced himself as a detective-sergeant from Scotland Yard. The manager seemed to resent his visit from the outset.

"Another of you!" he growled. "How many more detectives are coming here to waste my time? I've had three or four from the Borough Police already."

"I'm sorry, Mr. Yule, but without seeing you it is impossible to get much farther with an important case in London. You see, everything started with the theft of a pocket-book in the hall of your hotel."

"I don't believe that there was any theft at all; or anyway, if there was one, that it took place in this hotel. All you've got to go upon is a statement made by this Lieutenant Eccles that someone pinched a note-case out of the pocket of his overcoat hanging in the hall while he had lunch."

"Why do you doubt his word?"

"It's not the first time that that story has been told to me—people coming in and getting the run of their teeth, and then saying that their pockets have been picked, and that they've no money to pay for what they've had. And besides, Lieutenant Eccles didn't behave as a gentleman should behave...blustering in here and kicking up a row. When I told him that I couldn't be held responsible for things left in the hall, he said that he'd soon see whether I was responsible or not, and that he was going down to the police about me—for all the world as if he suspected me of stealing the thing. I tell you straight, I wasn't a bit surprised when the police found him in possession of a stolen car that very evening."

"Did nobody in the hotel notice a man tampering with the coats hanging in the hall?"

"No, if they had they would have told me."

It being obvious that nothing useful could be extracted from a man in that state of mind, Richardson's next visit was to the Chief Constable of the City Police—an officer who had worked his way up from the ranks and was genuinely anxious to help the sister force of the Metropolis. He was stout and rubicund.

"Glad to see you, sergeant. I was expecting somebody down from the Yard. Now what can I do for you?"

"I called, sir, to ask you whether you have had any line upon the man who is said by Lieutenant Eccles to have been posing as a detective of your Force."

"So far none at all. I didn't believe the story at first, but inquiry at a number of the public-houses facing the docks have made me change my opinion. In one of them—the Westward Ho—the barman remembered a man coming in and arresting a fellow who had been standing drinks; he resisted and it caused quite a row. But in the end the man went quietly. No arrest was made at that hour of the afternoon, and no one came to the station to report any arrest."

"Did the barman give a description of the sham detective?"

"None that could be of any use. I wish we could get one."

"I got a fair description of him from the porter at the Crown. Here it is just as I took it down."

The Chief Constable read it slowly until he came to the passage about the man's hands—"'A Londoner by his speech—hands rough, with short thick fingers—more like a man who's had rough work to do day after day.' Does that suggest anything to you, sergeant?"

"Yes, sir, it does. A man in regular employment doesn't throw up his work to pose as a detective."

"Exactly. That sort of man doesn't do any work unless he's made to. He lives by his wits. So, if that porter is right, the man we've got to look for is one who was doing rough work in some prison, and it must have been a convict prison, because they do not give their men rough work to do in local prisons. He must have been released quite recently from a convict prison where he worked either in the quarries or the stone-dressing parties. We seem to be getting warm. I dare say that if this description is sent to the Convict Supervision Office you could narrow down the inquiry to one out of a dozen possible men."

"That shall be done, sir. I suppose that you had no difficulty in identifying the stolen car?"

"None at all. The owner came crying down to us and gave us a description of it. Really he deserved to lose it for his carelessness in parking it where he did, but he's got it back now and the theft of his car doesn't help us at all, because no one saw it done. But the coincidence of that burglary and murder in Hampstead following close upon the theft of that pocket-book can scarcely have been an accident. There must be a gang, and one member of it may be an ex-convict. That's something to work on. If I hear anything useful I'll 'phone to Superintendent Foster at the Yard, and if you get any light from the Convict Supervision Office, you'll do the same by 'phoning to me."

Richardson's next visit was to the local superintendent of the County Constabulary, to whom he showed a copy of the woman's letter found in the pocket-book. The superintendent shook his head.

"As I read this letter, the writer is a farmer's wife, or a farmer on her own account, in urgent need of money. Well, sergeant, there are hundreds of little poultry farmers in my division round Portsmouth, and most, if not all of them, are in urgent need of money. No, sergeant; much as I should like to help you, it would be like looking for the proverbial needle in a bundle of hay, and a sheer waste of time and money to start an inquiry on nothing but this letter. If you had the envelope with a legible postmark something might be done."

"No, sir; as you see, there's no address and we haven't got the envelope. The letter was found in the pocket-book of Lieutenant Eccles, R.N.—found on the scene of the Hampstead murder—and he declines to say who wrote it."

"Is that the man who was arrested in Somersetshire for stealing a car in Portsmouth?"

"Yes, sir; the same man. I thought that perhaps one of your officers might know of some farmer who is in financial difficulties and might recognize the handwriting. We know that the writer lives quite close to the town."

"She talks of her place as a 'farm,' but probably it is nothing but an allotment with poultry running on it. After the war hundreds of ex-service men started poultry-keeping on little plots of land like that, expecting to make their fortunes. Most of them have gone under and the rest are on the verge of it. I could, of course, send an officer round the branch post offices in my division on the chance that one of their employees recognized the handwriting, but they aren't over-weighted with intelligence and I feel sure that it would be time wasted. I'm sorry." Not being authorized to part with the original letter, Richardson thanked him and took his leave. He had still one visit to make, but the sacred hour of lunch-time was approaching, when small business offices were bound to be closed. He had had no breakfast, and the void within him was affecting his spirits. He must eat and drink like other people, but he determined to turn his meal to account if he could. Not for him the amenities of the Crown Hotel or its like, where naval officers took their lady friends to lunch. He made for the Westward Ho public-house.

The company assembled at the bar-counter seemed to be in a convivial mood, but a hush fell when he entered the bar-room. One or two of the company gulped down the contents of their glasses and melted unostentatiously away. The rest stood their ground and eyed him with suspicion. Apparently it was his clothes that failed to please them.

"Looking for somebody, mister?" asked a burly dock-labourer with a red face, painted by some other agency than the sun.

"No, mate; I've come in here to get something to eat."

"Step into the bar-parlour, sir," suggested the barman, correctly interpreting the wishes of his clients. "I'll be along in two ticks."

Richardson passed through the door indicated and found himself alone in a tiny cubby-hole of a room. The door flew open behind him and the barman, in his shirt-sleeves, taking up a strategic position where he could take his guest's order and at the same time keep an eye upon his unguarded bar, asked him what he fancied.

"Cheese, bread and beer? That's easy. Got 'em all in the bar. Sit tight, sir, and I'll be back with them before you can turn round." He was as good as his word, and as he clapped down the plates and glass on the table and slipped back to the door, he remarked, "Took you for a 'tec, they did, in there. They're disputing now whether you belong to the City Force or the County."

"I suppose you get funny people in here sometimes and detectives pop in to have a look at them?"

"Funny people? You've said the word all right. Why, only a day or two ago a 'tec came in and arrested a bloke in that very room, and there was a bit of a rough-and-tumble over it right in the bar."

"The fellow resisted arrest, do you mean?"

"Yes, but only for a minute or two. He calmed down wonderful as soon as the 'tec slipped the darbies on 'im. I had my suspicions of the bloke before the 'tec came. He was too flush of money to be 'ealthy: started treating folks he'd never clapped eyes on before: wanted to treat me, too—"

"Did you let him?"

"Not much. I didn't like 'is looks or 'is ways—a little rat of a man, 'e was, with eyes that looked every way but straight at you, and what looked suspicious to me was that nobody in the bar knew 'im."

"And the detective? What was he like?"

"Oh, 'e was the real Mackay all right—same as you see on the pictures, stiff-built chap in a check suit and bowler 'at. But, Lord! It was as good as a play. The 'tec steps in at the door and starts looking round; the little bloke dives down and tries to hide his ugly mug behind the folks standing round 'im. The 'tec marches in, scatters the folks, and grips the little bloke by the arm, and 'e lets out a howl. 'I want you,' says the 'tec; 'you'd better come quiet or you'll be sorry after.' Then the fun began, right under my nose. One or two of the men looked ugly, but I told 'em that they'd be for it if they interfered with the police in the execution of their dooty, and they saw I was talking sense to them."

Richardson would have liked to prolong his conversation with the barman, but there was a call from the bar and the man left him at a run. He finished his meal and passed through the bar to pay his score, and went on his way.

A constable on point-duty directed him to Hampton Street, a gloomy little backwater retired from the stream of traffic. Mr. Moss conducted his business in a first-floor room which his clients reached by clambering up rickety and very dirty stairs. Mr. Moss was in keeping with his surroundings: he looked as if he needed soap and water even more acutely than his stairs. He might have pleaded lack of time for cleanliness, for year in and year out he was to be found sitting, bloated and obese, at his desk, like a spider waiting in his lair for the errant fly. At the moment he was consuming beef sandwiches from a greasy piece of newspaper, which he swept into a drawer on his left as Richardson opened the door. He received his visitor with an oily, professional grin and motioned him to a seat while he gulped down a mouthful of sandwich.

"What can I do for you, sir?" Richardson had not the appearance or the mien of a borrower.

"You *are* Mr. Moss? Before I tell you who I am, I should like you to read this letter."

Mr. Moss adjusted his spectacles and read the letter which had been found in Eccles' pocket-book. "Oh, I see. You are a gentleman from the Admiralty; but how did you know of the loan to Lieutenant Eccles? It's true that I threatened to tell the Admiralty, but I didn't do it; the threat was enough." He chuckled with self-satisfaction.

"I don't come from the Admiralty. I am a detective-sergeant from New Scotland Yard, and I want full information from you as to how this loan of seventy pounds was contracted."

"But why? The loan has been repaid and the interest too."

"When?"

"Three days ago Mr. Eccles repaid the loan and interest, and what seemed funny to me was that he paid it all in Treasury notes for one pound. It took me quite a while to count it over."

"Do you mean that he brought it himself?" Richardson had taken out his note-book.

"I didn't tell you that he brought it. He sent it by registered post."

"With a letter?"

"No, just a typewritten slip as far as I remember."

"Can you let me have that and the envelope?"

"I can, if I haven't thrown them both away." Mr. Moss began tossing the papers that littered his desk here and there. Then he seemed to have an inspiration. He waddled over to a box covered with dirty cretonne which he used instead of a waste-paper basket, and shovelled out its contents on to the floor. Digging in the mouldering pile of old sandwich-papers and refuse, he found at last what he wanted. Richardson, who had been waiting in some impatience, caught at the precious documents, smoothed them out and conveyed them to his pocket-book, after noting that the postmark was Chancery Lane and the date the day following the murder.

Chapter Seven

SUPERINTENDENT FOSTER took the train to Redford without expecting great results from his journey. The plaster casts of the footprints in the rose-bed were in his view the least important part of his quest: he wanted, if he could, to extract information from Jackson, the farmer, whether there were any Bank of England notes among the money he had paid for the farm, and whether he had recorded their numbers and any signatures that might be found on the back of some of them. Treasury notes, as he knew, could not be traced from their numbers. As it was important not to alarm the man by letting him think that he was in any way under suspicion, he had resolved to make that part of the inquiry first.

On alighting on the Redford platform, he allowed all the other passengers to pass out before him. Redford appeared to be one of those sleepy backwaters where everyone would be likely to know the business of all his neighbours: he put his first question to the ticket-collector. Yes, said that official, he knew Jackson's Farm.

"Is it an easy walk?"

"That depends on what you would call easy. It's a shade over a mile out of the town. There's taxis outside."

Foster looked at his watch. He could spare half an hour for the walk, and there was always the chance that he might encounter on the way somebody who might be induced to talk about Farmer Jackson. Having got his direction from the ticket-collector, he set out at a brisk walk, and it was not long before he came in sight of a stout woman going in the same direction. He put on speed and overtook her. She was a farmer's wife returning from the town loaded with parcels.

"Fine afternoon, madam," said Foster when he came up with her. "Can you tell me whether this road leads to Jackson's Farm?"

"That's right, sir. If you go straight on you'll get to the farm, but there's a short cut over the fields. I'm going that way myself and I'll show you."

"That's very kind of you. Let me carry some of those parcels for you."

Relieved of her parcels, the lady became more conversational. "You're acquainted with Mr. Jackson, sir?"

"No, I've never met him."

"Ah, then you've come down to see him on business. I can guess what it is. He told some of us that he'd bought his farm right out from the gentleman that owned it, and there's a lot of people hereabouts that didn't believe him. I believed him because I know from his wife that he's always been a saving man. He believed in no banks—changed all his money into notes and got her to sew them up in his mattress. She said that if one of them was missing he'd know it from the feel of the mattress when he went to bed."

"Then he's fond of money, you think?"

"Oh, that's no secret hereabouts—not that he's a miser by any means. He doesn't mind having to pay a good price for a good beast, but he's never been one to throw his money about— not he. What Edward Jackson don't know about farming isn't worth knowing, me husband says."

"I see. He's not one to throw his money away in public-houses?"

The lady laughed maliciously. "Not as a rule, like some do on market days, but there have been times—well, I mustn't tell tales—and Mr. Jackson has always been a good neighbour to us. Now, there's your stile, sir. You'll have three grass meadows to cross before you come to the farm, but in this weather you won't find any mud on the footpath."

Foster restored the parcels to their owner, thanked her, and crossed the stile. The country was looking its best for a tired Londoner on this glorious spring afternoon, and Foster was not insensible to its charm. He noted, too, all the evidences of sound farming in the meadows through which he passed—trimmed hedges, clean ditches and painted gates. He walked fast in his eagerness to see the man who had attained his heart's desire and become a freeholder. The gate of the third field opened into the farmyard where a farm-hand was feeding swill to the pigs.

"Is Mr. Jackson at home?" he asked.

"Aye, you'll find him round in the cow-house, milking."

Milking and ploughing, as Jackson afterwards assured him, were the jobs which he never entrusted to other hands. They were his hobby, because, as he said, you can run a cow dry in a week if you don't empty her udders.

There were twelve cows in the milking-byre, and Foster had to walk the length of it before he found his man. There on his stool he found a grey-haired man in his shirt-sleeves. "Mr. Jackson?" he asked.

"That's my name, sir," replied the man, without looking up.

"Can I have a word with you?"

"As many as you like when I've done my milking. This is my last cow and I can't knock off till she's done. I'll be with you directly if you like to go on to the house."

"Thank you, Mr. Jackson. I'll wait about outside till you've done."

This attention to detail, thought Foster, was the secret of Jackson's success in being able to buy his own farm. The farm-buildings were as well-cared for as the fields. They reminded him of his father's farm in Arbroath.

Five minutes later Jackson emerged from the byre, putting on his coat. "Now, sir," he said, "I'm at your service."

"I must explain that I'm a superintendent from Scotland Yard."

Jackson's face showed surprise, but no trace of alarm or confusion.

"I have a question or two to ask you about that money you paid over to Mr. MacDougal in Hampstead the other day."

"Come, you're not going to tell me that the sum wasn't right? Mr. MacDougal and I counted it over together."

"No, I've called to ask you whether there were any five-pound or ten-pound notes among the rest."

"Why come to me? Mr. MacDougal could have told you that."

"Didn't you see in the papers that there's been a burglary there the same night?"

Jackson gave a short laugh. "I've too much to do on my farm to have time to study the papers. I leave that to my missus. A burglary, was there?"

"Yes, and all that money was stolen."

Here Jackson's face did betray consternation. "Well, how does that affect me? I've got Mr. MacDougal's receipt for the money. He can't go back on the sale, can he?"

"I've come to you for information that may us to trace the thief. I've nothing to do with the sale and who stands to lose the money."

"I'd help you if I could, but the whole of the money was in Treasury notes. There wasn't a Bank of England note among them."

"Ah, that's a pity. Treasury notes are not like Bank of England notes which can be traced."

"Why can't you trace Treasury notes?"

"Because the banks don't keep a record of their numbers."

"That may be, but I don't trust my money to banks. More often than not when I put a note away I put my name on it, see? Just 'E. Jackson,' so's I'll know it again." A look of unspeakable cunning showed in his eyes.

Foster made a mental note of this information.

"Well, you'll be able to help me in one direction. We don't want people to start hinting that you went back to the house the same evening—"

Jackson's face reddened with anger. "Who's saying that? Tell me, and I'll cram the words down his throat."

"You've nothing to hide, Mr. Jackson, and the best way to stifle any talk of that kind is to agree to what I ask. You might let me see the boots you were wearing when you went to Mr. MacDougal's house to pay that money for the farm."

"My boots?" exclaimed Jackson in an astonishment that Foster felt sure was not feigned. "Why, I was wearing the boots I've got on me now. You see, five or six of us went up together to have a look at the beasts in Smithfield, and as there was likely to be mud about we went dressed as I am now—in our workaday clothes, if you know what I mean."

"You're sure that you were wearing these boots? Let me have a look at them."

"That's all very well, mister, but what's all this leading up to? Anyone would think that I was under suspicion of something."

"Nonsense. If you're under suspicion it isn't from me. I want to be in a position to clear you if any fool should start putting things about. Hold up your foot and let me look at the sole."

Still grumbling, Jackson put out one foot after the other and Foster examined the soles. The plate on the heel of the left foot had a piece missing as in Richardson's plaster cast, but Foster continued in his ordinary tone, "You've got another pair, I suppose."

"Yes, upstairs. But what's the game?"

"Only that I want you to lend me this pair for a day or so. I may want them to stop any gossip."

"Dang it: that's the limit. I'm not going to give any man my boots. I wonder at your asking such a thing."

"Come, Mr. Jackson, you must be reasonable. You don't want it to be said that you obstructed the police in the execution of their duty. That *would* set people talking. You shall have the boots back."

The obstinacy began to die out of Jackson's face. "All right, then, but I'll have to go indoors to change them."

He turned towards the house, but Foster detained him with another question. "Were you carrying a stick when you went to London?"

Jackson's eyes grew rounder with astonishment. "You'll be asking me next whether I was wearing kid gloves. Certainly I took a stick with me, and if you want to see it, come along to the house and I'll show it to you. The missus will be glad to give you a cup of tea while I'm changing my boots."

But Foster drew the line at accepting hospitality from a possible suspect. "No, thanking you all the same, Mr. Jackson, I won't come in. I can't spare the time. Just run in and change your boots, and bring the stick you took up to town that day with you."

Foster spent the next five minutes in watching the pigs squealing over their supper, and then Jackson reappeared with a neat brown-paper parcel containing his boots, and a straight walking-stick such as cattle-drovers use. It had no ferrule.

"Thank you, Mr. Jackson. I'll borrow this stick too, if you don't mind. You shall have it back tomorrow. I've only one or two more questions. You spent the night in London, I suppose?"

For the first time during the interview Jackson began to show symptoms of disquiet. "Yes, we all stayed in London until the morning."

"Where did you sleep?"

"Oh, at a little hotel. It was a poor little place, and it was so full that I had to share a room with another chap."

"Who was that?"

"Just a neighbour of mine—Joe Chapman is his name."

"Where does he live?"

"Just a little way down the road. You must have passed the farm coming here. But what's Joe Chapman got to do with this?"

"Nothing that I know of. I asked his address simply to use in case there was further gossip. Well, Mr. Jackson, I must not waste your time any longer. You shall have your boots and stick back in a day or two. I'm much obliged to you. Good afternoon."

In leaving the farm, Foster abandoned short cuts over fields and went into the high road, where in the first hundred yards he had the good fortune to encounter a postman on his afternoon round.

"Mr. Joseph Chapman, sir?" he said. "You'll find the farm about a hundred yards on the way you're going—on the right. You can't miss it."

The farm was of old red brick: the farm-house looked very neat and tidy with its steps new-whitened and curtains in the windows. Foster rang the bell, and straightway found himself face to face with an old acquaintance—the farmer's wife whose parcels he had carried for her.

"Glad to see you, sir. You've just come in time for a cup of tea. Did you find Mr. Jackson all right?"

"Thanks to you, madam, I did. You are Mrs. Chapman, are you not? I called to have a word or two with your husband."

"You'll excuse me asking, sir, but are you the new insurance agent?"

"No, madam," laughed Foster; "I've not come to worry you with business. I want to ask Mr. Chapman a question or two about his recent visit to London."

The lady's curiosity took fire; it would have been volcanic if she had known that she was speaking to an officer from Scotland Yard. Foster was quick to see her curiosity and to ascribe it to its actual cause—the fact that her husband had been less communicative about his adventures in London than she considered she had a right to expect.

"Won't you come in and sit down, sir? My husband is somewhere about. I'll send one of my girls to fetch him in. Bella!" she cried.

A flapper of fifteen, as solidly built as her mother, came running from the dairy.

"Run and tell your Dad that there's a gentleman here waiting to see him. Tell him he's to come just as he is. Kindly step this way, sir."

She led Foster into a sitting-room, evidently reserved for guests of distinction, such as the parson or the squire. It was painfully tidy and unlived in, and the colours of the upholstery swore with the paper and with each other. The problem was how to secure five minutes alone with the husband without shattering the domestic peace of the household by appearing to have secrets with him which the wife was not to share. He had little time for making up his mind how to act, for hard upon the heels of the flapper daughter with the teapot followed her father—a jolly, round and ruddy farmer in his shirt-sleeves. When the introductions were made, Foster took his decision in a flash. There must be no secrets.

"Bella tells me that you were the gentleman who helped the Missus home with her parcels this afternoon, sir. I thought it was my neighbour Jackson you were going to see."

"I've seen him, thank you, Mr. Chapman, and now—only one lump, please—and now I've come on to see you. Wonderful scones these, Mrs. Chapman. I haven't tasted better since I left Scotland. I'll bet that you baked them yourself."

The lady blushed with pleasure. "Sit down, Dad, and drink your tea like a Christian."

"Oughtn't I to have a wash first?"

"Not a bit of it. If this gentleman don't mind, I'm sure I don't. He's never told me his name."

"Foster—Charles Foster, madam. But really, I oughtn't to be spoiling your tea-party by talking business."

"Take your tea into the kitchen, Bella. We're going to talk business—your Dad and me and this gentleman."

The girl snatched a couple of buttered scones from the dish and went off with a rebellious expression, leaving Foster to open his business.

"I must begin by telling you that I'm a detective-superintendent from Scotland Yard." He felt, rather than saw, the effect produced by this announcement. "I want you, Mr. Chapman, to help me over a rather difficult case, if you will. I understand that on the night you spent in London last week the hotel was so crowded that you had to share a room with Mr. Jackson."

"Oh, he told you that, did he? I should have thought that he'd like to forget about it."

"Why? Did you have a disturbed night?"

Chapman burst into a laugh. "A disturbed night is a mild thing to call it. I suppose, Mr. Foster, that anything I tell you will be treated confidential. You see, my neighbour Jackson is Vicar's churchwarden, and it would cause a world of trouble if it got out. Jackson had bought his own farm that afternoon and nothing would satisfy him but to celebrate the occasion. He's not a drinking man, and I suppose he doesn't carry liquor well for that reason. Anyway, we had an awful job with him getting him safe to the hotel, and there was a room short. As none of the others would have him in with them, I helped him upstairs to my room and gave him the bed while I dossed down in the chair for a sleep. Lord! Mr. Foster, you've never heard Jackson sing, have you? No, of course you haven't. His 'Amen' in church after each prayer is nothing to his singing, nor the hyena-house at feeding-time at the Zoo neither. I tried my hardest to get him to drop singing hymns, but he wouldn't, and then all of a sudden he stopped, rolled off the bed and stuck his hat on. By that time he had sobered down a bit. He kept feeling in his pockets and muttering, 'I've left my money somewhere.' I told him to lie down and sleep, but he wouldn't listen to me—just sticks his hat on his head wrong side before, and clatters down the stairs into the street. It wasn't safe to let him go out like that, and I had to go after him, if only to save him from getting run over."

"Did you catch up with him?" asked Foster.

"No, because he started running. I never knew before how a drunken man could run, but I managed to keep him in sight as the streets were pretty empty; and a fine dance he led me! Street after street we went through until we came to a street of big houses standing back in gardens. He went through the gate of one of them."

"You didn't notice the name of the street?"

"No, I didn't. It was too dark to read names. I stayed by the gate to see what he'd do, and saw him floundering about among the flowers. He picked himself up though, and the next thing I saw was him standing on the doorstep, pulling at the bell. I could hear it ringing from where I was standing, but nobody came. So then I went in and got him by the arm and asked him what he thought he was doing, ringing folks up after midnight. He began to cry then, and said that he'd spent a lifetime saving up that money, and that he was sure he'd left it in the house and the people wouldn't open the door."

"Was he carrying a walking-stick when he went out?"

"Yes, he'd taken my stick instead of his own when he went out, and it was all I could do to get it back from him. Luckily for us, an empty taxi overtook us, and I shouted to the driver. That's how I got him back to the hotel."

"He'd sobered down?"

"Yes, he was crying like a child in the taxi until he fell asleep. It cost me four and nine, did that journey, but what could I do? He's paid me back since, but to this day he says he doesn't remember a thing about it."

"You got your stick back though. Can I see it?"

"Certainly you can. Fetch it from the lobby, Mother, will you?"

Mrs. Chapman went out for the stick—a stick with a crook handle. Foster took it with a smile and examined the ferrule, which was much worn down on the side opposite to the crook.

"You have no luck with this stick, Mr. Chapman. I'm going to ask you for the loan of it for a day or two."

Mrs. Chapman was bursting to ask the reason for this strange request, but Foster forestalled the question.

"It's to clear Mr. Jackson of any suspicion, madam. There was a burglary in that house that night, and we've come across marks in the flowerbeds that might have been made by the burglar, but which this stick may explain away. You shall have the stick back without fail."

"Did the burglar get away with Mr. Jackson's money?" asked the lady, round-eyed with horror.

"I'm afraid that he did."

Here was material for exciting gossip for a fortnight if she dared to use it, but her husband foresaw the danger. "Not a word of this to any of the neighbours, Mother, or you'll end by setting poor Jackson against us. Not a word, eh?"

Mrs. Chapman drew herself up. "Have you ever known me to gossip, Dad? What do you take me for?"

Foster took leave of his host and hostess with mutual expressions of goodwill. The last he heard of them was a jocose injunction from the farmer to be sure and not leave his stick in the train.

Foster was doing well in his favourite process of elimination. All the marks in the front garden were now innocently accounted for, and he smiled as he thought of his next interview with Richardson on the subject of the little holes left in the soft earth of the rose-beds, which he had noticed while his subordinate was pouring plaster of Paris into the footprints. They did not teach everything in the detective class of which Richardson had been such an assiduous member; for example, they had not taught him that a straight walking-stick wears evenly all round the ferrule, whereas a stick with a crook handle wears down on the side opposite the crook.

This had been puzzling him ever since he had examined the ferrule of Jackson's stick, for the holes he had examined had all been made by a ferrule worn down on the side towards the toes of the footprints. Farmer Chapman had furnished him with the explanation: Jackson had borrowed his stick. Foster's satisfaction was natural. There had been no detective class in his young days: every detective had had to accumulate the science of clues by hard experience, and this was one of his own discovery, or so he believed.

Chapter Eight

RICHARDSON was at his table in the detective-sergeants' room, writing his report of his visit to Portsmouth when Willis, Charles Morden's messenger, came in with an air of business about him. He looked at the bowed heads at the tables and made a bee-line for Richardson's.

"Here's a little job for you, Richardson. Mr. Foster's out, and there's a gent in with Mr. Morden who wants a statement taken from him."

Richardson pushed back his papers with an air of resignation. "Can't the man write down what he has to say? One of these time-wasters, I suppose."

"Mr. Morden is sending him to you because he's brought some information about the Hampstead murder—at least that's what I gathered from what he was saying to the gent when I answered his bell. Take care that your head doesn't get too big for your hat. He said, 'I'll get you to tell all this to one of the officers engaged on the case. He's a junior, but he's about the smartest junior I've got.' Put that in your pipe and smoke it, and never call him a time-waster again. He's a barrister."

"Right, bring him in, but I wish to God Mr. Foster was here to deal with him."

Willis retired and returned almost immediately with Dick Meredith, who appeared disconcerted when he found himself in a room with five detectives, all busily writing.

"This is Sergeant Richardson, sir," said Willis, bringing him up to the table.

"Good morning, sergeant. Look here, can't we have a room somewhere, just you and I?"

"Is there anyone in the waiting-room, Willis?" asked Richardson.

"No, you could have that to yourselves."

"You see, sir, we are growing out of this building already," apologized Richardson as he gathered up writing materials. "If you don't mind a small room we shall be alone there."

He led the visitor along the passage to a tiny room on the left of the main entrance. They sat down on opposite sides of a little table.

Dick Meredith opened his business. "I must begin by telling you that I have been instructed to represent Lieutenant Eccles in the police-court proceedings at Bridgwater—for being in possession of a stolen car and assaulting the police."

"Yes, sir?" Richardson's heart had missed a beat, but his manner remained that of the polite listener. "I did not hear your name, sir?"

"Richard Meredith: you'll find it in the Law List. Mr. Morden told me that you were engaged on a case of burglary and murder in Hampstead, and I have brought you something which is not a clue, of course, but may be of interest to you nevertheless." Dick took a folded newspaper from his pocket and opened it out. "Mr. Eccles tells me that the man who induced him to enter that stolen car, and posed as a detective, was carrying this in his pocket and left it on the driving-seat when he absconded. You will see that one of the paragraphs is marked in blue pencil—presumably by a member of the gang."

Richardson read the paragraph carefully, and looked up with inquiry in his eyes. "Can you suggest any connection between the marking of this paragraph and the Hampstead case, sir?"

"No, I confess that it beats me, but I think that you ought to keep the paper in case some connection turns up later."

"I will, sir. One never knows in such a case as this what may turn up. It's an awkward mix-up for Lieutenant Eccles."

"It is, because the murder took place in his uncle's house; but there is another coincidence, though a slender one. It was about that coincidence that Mr. Morden asked me to make a statement. The story reached me through a personal friend, and therefore at this stage it is only second-hand."

"It would be more regular, sir, if your friend would come here and make the statement."

"I couldn't get him to do that, but later on I will bring him to confirm it. Perhaps you will take it down."

Thereupon Dick Meredith related what his Canadian friend, Jim Milsom, had told him. He was surprised to see the pencil poised in the air almost before he had completed a sentence: Richardson was equally impressed with the succinctness of the story as told by a man with legal training. There was not a word too much or too little. Only at one point did he show that he was more than a mechanical amanuensis.

"Excuse me, sir. By 'Ralph Lewis' do you mean the young politician whose name is given in this newspaper?"

"Yes, that's the man. No doubt he can take care of himself, but there would be a great outcry if this Canadian monomaniac were to shoot him. The uncomfortable part of the business is that the man has disappeared."

"Disappeared, sir?"

"Yes; my informant tells me that he rang up the hotel and they told him that his luggage is there, but they haven't seen him for six days, and he hasn't paid his bill."

Richardson smiled. "That often happens, sir. When visitors to London run short of money they have a way of walking off and leaving the hotel proprietor to pay himself out of the luggage if he can."

"Quite so, but my friend says that this man would never have gone off without letting him know; that if he had run short of money he would have borrowed from him enough to pay his bill. The people you speak of are those that have no friends in London."

Richardson was busily writing down this last statement. "Then, sir, for all your friend knows to the contrary this man may be in London at this moment?"

"He may, and I think you will agree that it is always better to prevent a crime than to arrest the criminal after he has committed it."

"Quite so, sir. I shall pass on your statement at once, and I have no doubt that some action will be taken. If you hear anything of this man, Moore, I hope that you will let us know. I suppose that you feel confident that Lieutenant Eccles will be discharged at the preliminary hearing, or at any rate that if he is committed for trial he will be granted bail?"

"I hope to get him discharged, perhaps with a fine for the assault. In any case he will be granted bail. Have you anything fresh to tell me that would be helpful?"

"I was down at Portsmouth yesterday, sir. The result of my inquiries there was to bear out Mr. Eccles' story. That is all that I can tell you at the moment, sir. It would have helped us if Mr. Eccles had told us frankly who it was that he went to see during the morning of the day he was arrested, but he would not."

"He has not told me either, but he assured me that it had nothing whatever to do with the case. Well, I mustn't keep you, sergeant. Thank you for taking down my statement so accurately. I dare say we shall meet again in the course of the case."

"I hope so, sir."

As Richardson was returning to the detective-sergeants' room, with the marked newspaper in his hand, he encountered Foster in the corridor. "I'm glad you're back, sir," he said.

"What's that you have in your hand, young man?"

"I've just been taking a statement from Eccles' counsel. He left this paper with me."

"Step in here, my boy," said Foster, leading the way into the superintendents' room, "and let me hear what you've been doing, but tell me first whether they taught you anything about the prints of walking-sticks in that detective class of yours."

Richardson knew his chief in this humour and guessed that he had scored a small success off his own bat. He searched his memory. "No, sir, I don't think they did."

"They didn't tell you the difference between the marks made in soft ground by the points of straight sticks and sticks with a crook handle? I guessed as much. Well—while you were down at Portsmouth I ran up to Redford and cleared up the mystery of these marks you found in the rose-beds in Laburnum Road. They were made by Jackson, the farmer, who was coming back for his money when he was almost too drunk to stand, and it was the prints of his stick that proved it."

"So we can rule him out, sir?"

"We can. You'll read it in my report. Now what about your visit to Portsmouth?"

"I've only a few words to add to my report, and you shall have it on your table in the next few minutes."

"Have you taken Eccles out of the picture too?"

"Yes, Mr. Foster—except for one thing. The loan he had from the money-lender was repaid on the day after the murder."

"Repaid? Aye, but this is serious. No one would have repaid it but himself, or—"

"Or the man who stole his pocket-book, Mr. Foster. You will remember that the money-lender's letter was in the flap of the pocket-book."

Foster was plunged in thought. "It's not like any burglar that I know to pay out a cool seventy pounds from his booty when he could safely have stuck to it. The plot's thickening."

"Yes, sir, it is. I'd like you to read this statement I've just taken from Eccles' counsel, Mr. Meredith. He left this newspaper with me: Eccles told him that the sham detective left it in the car. I shall finish my report while you're reading it."

Foster read the statement with a puckered brow, and then carried that and the newspaper to Charles Morden's room.

"I understand that you saw a barrister named Meredith this morning, sir, and that you sent him on to Sergeant Richardson to take his statement."

"I did. What he told me seemed to have some slight bearing on the Hampstead murder, and you were out of the office at the time. Is this the statement?"

"Yes, sir. There is nothing in the newspaper that will help me, but the rest of the statement might be a matter for the Special Branch."

"You mean as to giving protection to this Mr. Ralph Lewis? Really, Mr. Foster; if we are to give protection to every young gentleman who practises the art of self-advertisement, where is it to stop?"

"Quite so, sir, but if a crack-brained gunman from over the water puts a bullet into him in mistake for another man, and it comes out at the inquest that we were warned of his danger, there might be trouble."

"You think that Mr. Lewis may have a double? It's possible. Our fingerprint people have quite a collection of 'doubles' who look identical in their photographs, but have quite different fingerprints. No doubt you have seen them."

"Yes, sir, I have, but according to this statement this Moore seems to be a dangerous man."

"Very well, then, let us send Richardson to attend the Albert Hall meeting and arrange with the stewards to find him a seat on the platform where he can get a good view of the audience. He can wait at the private door until Lewis arrives, follow him in, and perhaps have a word with him after the meeting."

"Yes, sir, but we might be too late. Suppose that this gunman is lying in wait for him at the platform entrance."

"True. I suppose that it would be wise to get F Division to send a C.I.D. patrol to the platform entrance until Lewis is safely into the hall. You had better 'phone the superintendent."

"Very good, sir."

"Of course if Richardson spots any doubtful character among the audience he will know what to do. We will be guided by his report before we give regular police protection to Lewis. How are you getting on with the Hampstead murder?"

"Slowly, sir. You'll see the reports presently. We have been able to rule out one of the possible suspects, but we can't yet eliminate Lieutenant Eccles because Richardson found that his loan from the money-lender was repaid on the day following the murder."

"The devil it was! Does Eccles admit paying it?"

"He's not been asked yet, sir, but he had so good an alibi in a police cell in Somersetshire, that as the money was repaid on the morning following the murder, it couldn't have been Eccles who repaid it. It can only have been the man who stole the pocket-book."

"H'm! One would have said that he has some personal enemy who wanted to shift the blame on to him."

"Yes, sir, or wanted to get him out of the way."

"The man must have thought out his plan weeks ahead: it couldn't have been made up on the spur of the moment after reading the contents of the pocket-book. The man must have been watching the movements of the *Dauntless* for days before she came in. Did Richardson find out anything else in Portsmouth?"

"Yes, sir, he got a good description of the false detective and passed it on to the Chief Constable of Portsmouth. I think we shall find as we go on that we are dealing with a gang with a very warm man at the head of it. I believe that it will turn out to have been this man who actually committed the murder, and that he was alarmed by that old farmer, Jackson, ringing the front-door bell just when he had shot the woman and stolen the money. We know that Jackson went back to the house after midnight with a drunkard's idea of getting back his money. You'll read it all in our reports this afternoon."

"Good! After I've read them I should like to have another talk about the case."

A few minutes later Richardson took his finished report to the superintendents' room and found Foster alone.

"We've a job for you, young man. Mr. Morden is fighting shy of putting this Mr. Lewis under protection until we know a little more. He wants you to attend that meeting in the Albert Hall and keep your eyes open. I'll arrange with the stewards to give you a seat on the platform. When Lewis leaves the hall you'll tell him who you are and get as much out of him as you can."

"Very good, sir. I quite understand."

"I've been thinking about that newspaper, said to have been left in the stolen car. It's a curious coincidence that this man, Moore, should be looking for Ralph Lewis, and that a member of this gang—if there is a gang—should be carrying a paper in which Ralph Lewis's name is marked in blue pencil. Doesn't it look as if there were some connection between the gang and the man Mr. Meredith calls 'Poker' Moore?"

"That has struck me too, sir."

"We ought to find out whether there is any connection between Ralph Lewis and Eccles. When you attend that meeting at the Albert Hall that is one of the things you might ask Ralph Lewis."

"What puzzles me, sir, is why anyone wants to murder Lewis. It isn't a crime to want to be a successful politician. If you've nothing else for me to do now, I thought of running out to Hampstead to see Lieutenant Eccles and hear what he has to say about the repayment of that seventy pounds to the money-lender in Portsmouth."

"Yes, that's the first thing to do, and then you might find out whether he has ever met Ralph Lewis."

When he called at the house in Laburnum Road Richardson was fortunate enough to find Ronald Eccles at home. The young man received him in his uncle's library, and was perfectly friendly. "What's gone wrong now?" were his first words.

"I've been down to Portsmouth to make inquiries, sir. I found the money-lender from whom you obtained a loan of seventy pounds."

It was impossible not to notice the change of colour at this announcement, or the change in manner. Eccles was now definitely on the defensive. Richardson proceeded suavely, "He told me that the loan had been repaid on the morning after the murder—repaid all in Treasury notes that came with a typed slip—'In repayment of Mr. Eccles' loan.' I have the slip here, sir, if you would like to see it."

"How do you mean—repaid? Who sent the money?"

"That is what I came to ask you, sir," replied Richardson blandly. The young man's agitation had not escaped him, but at this stage he could not say whether it was due to surprise, or to some guilty knowledge.

"If you think it was me, you are barking up the wrong tree. How could I repay it? I hadn't the money."

"Can you suggest who could have any interest in repaying it except yourself?"

"No, how the devil can I?—unless it was the blighter who stole my pocket-book and broke into my uncle's house."

"Have you a typewriter in the house? I ask only to be in a position to clear the matter up."

"Yes, I believe that my uncle has one. I'll go and get it."

He returned two minutes later carrying a portable typewriter—a Corona.

Richardson took off the cover and sat down before it. He copied the communication he had got from the money-lender and compared the two. He smiled to himself. "It's a curious coincidence that both these copies were made with a Corona with the same fount of type, sir, but they were not made with the same machine. The letter to the money-lender was made with a modern machine: yours is an old machine. You can see the difference for yourself. The 'e' in 'repayment' is quite out of alignment: so is the 'o' in 'loan' and the 's' in 'Eccles.'"

"But I can see that you still think that I wrote this slip."

"No, Mr. Eccles; there can be no harm in my telling you that I don't. What is puzzling us is why anyone should be trying to injure you. Have you any enemy?"

"Not that I know of. I've had rows with people, of course. Who hasn't? But I can't think of anyone who would do a thing like this."

"I understand that the man who drove you off in a stolen car left a newspaper behind him with a passage marked in it."

"He did. The passage was something about a political meeting."

"Mr. Meredith left the paper with us. The speaker at the meeting was to be Mr. Ralph Lewis. May I ask whether you know that gentleman?"

"I've never heard of him."

"Thank you, Mr. Eccles. I can be quite frank with you. There is nothing now in your statement that is not borne out by evidence, except the question where you spent the morning before lunching at the Crown Hotel. If you could tell us that in confidence the whole of the case, as it affects you, would be cleared up." While he was speaking Richardson saw the young man's face redden with anger.

"I've told you already that that has nothing whatever to do with the case."

"If you told me in confidence, I could promise you that it wouldn't go any farther."

For a moment Ronald Eccles seemed to hesitate. Then he tossed back his head defiantly. "I've told you that I want to help the police all I can, but they have no right to cross-examine me about my private affairs. You can do what you like, but where I went before the trouble began is nobody's business but my own."

"Very well, Mr. Eccles. I won't detain you any longer. Thank you for what you have told me."

From Hampstead Richardson returned to the office, but not to his own room. He went up to the Convict Supervision Office upstairs, and drew one of the sergeants aside. To him he explained what he was looking for.

"An ex-convict who poses as a detective. We'll have a look in the Crime Index." He went to a card-index. "Here we are. Seven of them. You can take your choice." He handed the seven cards to Richardson, who ran through them rapidly. Six of them had escaped penal servitude and had served short terms in a local prison, but the seventh had committed a serious theft while posing as a detective officer, and this was his second offence of personation. He had been sentenced at Liverpool to three years' penal servitude.

"You don't happen to know whether he has lately been discharged?"

"Let us have a look at the card. Yes, if he earned his maximum remission, Richard Hathaway would have been let loose on the world a month ago."

"Of course you would not know whether he has been reporting to the police. If he came out a month ago, he ought to have reported twice."

"I can't tell you that off-hand. I shall have to ask the people downstairs, nor can I tell you how he was employed in the convict prison. You'll have to look at his penal record over the way." He jerked his thumb in the direction of the Home Office in Whitehall.

Richardson stopped at the office downstairs on his way and ascertained that Hathaway had reported himself once, immediately after his discharge, but had since dispensed with the formality; that he had joined the Royal Aid Society and that the last report from its secretary was to the effect that he had been evasive about the work offered him, and that the Society had since lost sight of him. Hathaway, therefore, was liable to arrest for failing to report to the police.

Richardson had already been to the Convict Registry in the Home Office and knew the Registrar personally. Hathaway's penal record was placed on the table before him, and he was free to see how he conformed with the description given him by the porter in the hotel in Portsmouth. He was surprised to find how the description fitted the man whose photograph, full face and profile, was gummed to the second page of the thick foolscap record. Then he turned to the page showing the nature of his employment. In the sheet recording his applications to the governor there were three applications for the stone-dressing party in fairly quick succession; the governor had at last succumbed to his importunity and had noted his name for the party. Thereafter he did not trouble the governor again and must have attained his heart's desire, for there were no further entries. His conduct throughout his sentence had been exemplary, with the exception of one report for persistent talking, for which he received a caution, but lost no marks: he attained the maximum remission of his sentence and was discharged to the care of the Discharged Prisoners' Aid Society.

Richardson made copious notes from the document, recording Hathaway's height, weight and age. He knew that he could get a photograph of him and his fingerprints at Scotland Yard, on the other side of the street. Armed with these, he could see Lieutenant Eccles again and get from him a provisional identification pending Hathaway's arrest after the usual request for his arrest had been circulated to all police forces in the *Police Gazette*.

He had one other visit to make. The Prisoners' Aid Society, which was subsidized by Government, had its office near Charing Cross, little more than a stone's-throw away. There he was fortunate enough to find the very agent who had had an interview with Hathaway on his discharge from Dartmoor.

"Richard Hathaway?" the agent exclaimed, laughing. "Do I remember him? I should think I did. He was a card—that man. I should be sorry for the donkey who valued his hind leg when Hathaway started to talk to him."

"He could talk?"

"Could he not? I told him that he had mistaken his vocation; that he'd better give up crime and take to selling oil shares if he wouldn't take the job of road-mending that we were able to offer him. It wasn't work he wanted from us: all he wanted was his gratuity in full, and when I told him that our rules were against him, he told me what he thought of us, and I had to threaten to call a constable."

"Where is he now is what I want to know."

"So do we. I've still got the balance of his gratuity in this drawer. As to *where* he is, I can tell you the place where you *won't* find him, and that's Liverpool, the place where he was convicted. The police up there know him too well by sight after he posed as one of their detectives. He wouldn't think Liverpool a healthy town for him."

"Could he have gone abroad, do you think?"

"If he could steal some other man's passport he might, but I rang up the Passport Office some days ago to put them wise about him in case he applied for one."

Richardson dined frugally and quickly before taking the Tube again for Hampstead. He calculated that Eccles would be dining with his uncle and that he might catch him before he went out. He was right. He was shown into the library as before. Two minutes later Eccles came in, with a shade of annoyance and surprise on his face.

"I'm sorry to have to trouble you again, sir, but the matter is rather urgent. I have a photograph to show you and I should be glad if you would look at it carefully before committing yourself to an opinion." He handed him the portrait of Hathaway.

Eccles reddened as he examined it and his breath came quicker.

"By the Lord, sergeant, you've got him! That's the blighter who said he was a detective and got me into this mess."

"We haven't arrested him yet, sir. When we do, we shall have to ask you to come down and pick him out from a dozen other men."

"I'll come down all right, but I won't promise to keep my hands off him when I do identify him."

Chapter Nine

SERGEANT RICHARDSON arrived at the door which gave access to the platform of the Albert Hall a quarter of an hour before the advertised time, and sought the steward who had charge of the privileged seats on the platform. He found that the seat reserved for him was placed at the back.

"I thought that you would not wish to be too much in evidence," the official explained, "but of course you can sit wherever you think it would be most useful for your purpose."

"I should not get a good view of the audience from the back," said Richardson. "If it is all the same to you, I should prefer to sit here." He pointed to the end of the second row of chairs.

"I hope that you have no reason to fear any disturbance?" The poor steward was evidently on tenterhooks.

"Indeed I hope not, but it is always well to be prepared in these big public meetings. Do you expect a large audience?"

"In the body of the hall, yes. Practically every seat has been booked. One cannot tell beforehand about the gallery."

Richardson glanced at his watch.

"Yes," said the steward, "I think that we had better be moving. The platform people ought to be at the door in five minutes."

Richardson's first concern on passing out of the building was to satisfy himself that no suspicious-looking person was waiting for the arrivals. He nodded to a detective from F Division who was, as he knew, present on the same quest. Then he strolled over to the uniformed constable on duty and made himself known as a comrade in plain clothes.

"Expecting a dust-up in the hall, are you?" asked the constable.

"Not a big disturbance, but there may be an attempt at assaulting the speaker, and if there is, I may have to call you in to lend me a hand inside."

"Right oh, I'll stand by, but look here, if anyone is going to start spoiling the manly beauty of 'Love's Young Dream,' why not let them fight it out? It would do the young gentleman a world of good."

"It might, but if he starts on the job with a revolver..."

"Oh, that's the game? Right oh!"

The constable might have said more, but at that moment a car drew up at the door and stewards crowded round to greet the occupant—a well-known politician who had a weakness for presiding at public meetings. Richardson heard him ask whether "our speaker" had arrived. Two ladies, the Chairman's wife and daughter, were helped out of the car; they were ushered into the waiting-room. The car moved on.

Two minutes later another car discharged its occupants—a Member of Parliament, accompanied by three ladies—and then came a humble taxi with a single occupant—a young man of about thirty. This was the man they were all waiting for—Mr. Ralph Lewis—the hero of the evening. He was ushered in, with Richardson in his wake. It was three minutes to eight.

The Chairman welcomed him cordially, though Richardson, who was watching his reception through the open doorway, doubted whether he had ever seen him before. Presentations to the other platform people having been made, the Chairman looked at his watch and pronounced it to be time to move to the platform. Richardson attached himself to the tail of the procession.

A burst of applause from the hall was borne to his ears as the Chairman and the speaker reached their chairs. He went unobserved to his seat and found himself gazing at a sea of faces, mostly feminine. As his eyes became accustomed to the light, he saw that there were men as well as women, but that whereas the women's faces were alive with curiosity and interest, the men who had been dragged to the meeting as their escort, looked dull, bored and contemptuous. As the steward had predicted, every seat on the floor of the vast building seemed to be occupied, but in the galleries the audience was restricted to a sparsely filled row or two in the front.

The Chairman was on his feet, booming platitudes in a voice trained to reach the farthest recesses of the hall. He was giving the audience a life-sketch of the speaker who was to follow him, founded, no doubt, on the ample material furnished by the gentleman himself to the editors of *Who's Who*; but no one appeared to be listening to him, and when he sat down after delivering a very sanguine prediction about the after-career of political distinction which was awaiting Mr. Ralph Lewis, there was a stir of relief in the hall.

Then Ralph Lewis rose to his feet and there was a silence that could be felt. He was tall, slim and very good-looking, with dark hair, which he had allowed to grow too long, and well-marked eyebrows which would become bushy when he grew older, and white and regular teeth. His claim to hold audiences rested in his voice—the voice of a man who might have become a great singer—melodious, vibrant and cultivated. He seemed to be entirely at his ease as he began his speech in a low tone which carried, nevertheless, to the farthest limits of the great building. He had the trick of happy phrasing, of raising a laugh by a clever epigram, of striking an appropriate note of pathos as he described the unhappy state of his less fortunate fellow-countrymen who were tramping day after day to the Labour Exchanges in search of work through no fault of their own. The unemployed are, as has been observed, a godsend to the rising politician, because in championing their cause it is not necessary to attack anybody but the World Economic Crisis, which, having no soul to save or body to kick, cannot hit back.

Richardson's attention began to wander from the speech while his eye travelled along the rows of seats in search of a familiar face, but the music of the voice, as it rose and fell, continued to exercise its magnetic influence on him. The first row below the platform was occupied by reporters, either writing or gazing with indifference at the speaker. It was not until his eye was sweeping the fifth row that it caught a face that he knew—the barrister who was to defend Lieutenant Eccles, Mr. Meredith, whose statement he had taken a few hours before. In contrast with the face of the lady sitting beside him, his expression was critical and cold: clearly the magnetic voice was powerless to move him, but that might have been said of many of the males among the audience.

The speaker had been on his feet for nearly half an hour before Richardson began to realize that if he had been called upon for a condensed report on the subject of his speech, he would not know what to say. There were plenty of fireworks; the speaker seemed to be in deadly earnest; clearly he had captured his audience, since every gem of oratory was interrupted by spontaneous applause. He had all the tricks of the trained orator, waiting with poised hand until the applause died down, picking up the thread of his discourse without a check. He spoke without notes, even scribbled on his shirt-cuff, and he never repeated himself. But though he held up many of our cherished institutions to scorn, though he deplored the lack of leadership in the nation that was needed to bring her out of the difficulties, as far as Richardson was able to judge, he made no practical suggestion as to the policy that such a leader should adopt if he could be found. It was a magnificent oratorical effort, but it left all those questions in the air.

He had tossed his mane in a stirring passage and had paused before sinking his wonderful voice almost to a whisper, and was proceeding to draw a picture of England as he would have her, when quite suddenly there was a change. His voice failed him in the middle of a sentence; he clutched at the back of his chair to steady himself; he had turned as white as paper. Following the direction of his eyes, Richardson saw that they were fixed upon a man in the third row who had half risen from his seat and was staring fixedly at the speaker.

He was not the only person in the vast audience who had risen. The Chairman was up and had thrown an arm round Lewis's shoulders; a little man came hurrying along the gangway to the platform and was heard to call out, "I am a doctor. Can I be of any use?" The Chairman beckoned to him and he ran up the steps to the platform and quickly took charge of the proceedings. Ralph Lewis was half led, half carried into the waiting-room, and the Chairman briefly announced in an appropriate tone that, owing to sudden illness, the distinguished speaker had been forbidden on medical advice to conclude his magnificent speech. The audience began to disperse in a confused babble of conversation.

Richardson's first impulse was to jump from the platform and head off the man who, as he now felt sure, had caused the speaker to break down, but he found it impossible to break through the solid mass of humanity that blocked the gangway: the people could not make way for him if they would. Feeling certain that he could recognize the man, he slipped out behind the platform and ran round to the main entrance, only to discover that the audience was streaming out from several exit doors, and that, in the feeble light from the street lamps, it would be impossible, except by a miracle, to recognize any individual in the crowd. There was nothing for it but to get back to the waiting-room and have speech with Ralph Lewis if he could. He was not too late. He found the sick man reclining in an armchair, drinking some potion administered by the doctor, from a tumbler brought from the platform, while the Chairman was playing the heavy father, and his womenkind were fluttering in the background. He drew the doctor aside, explained who he was, and asked his permission to see his patient home. The doctor said that he understood that the Chairman intended to drive him home in his car.

"Is he seriously ill?" asked Richardson.

"I don't think so," replied the doctor. "His heart is a little jumpy, but I can discover nothing organically wrong with him. If I didn't know who he was, I should have said that he was suffering from nothing worse than a bad shock or a fright, but of course in his case that's absurd. Like all these public speakers, he lives on his nerves. If he goes quietly to bed and isn't worried in any way, he'll be all right in the morning."

After this medical warning, Richardson understood that he could not, in decency, force his conversation on the patient, and he set off to walk home. He was rehearsing in his mind the personal description of the man whose look alone had been sufficient to cause this facile speaker to break down. "About five feet eleven inches in height—slim in body, but rather broad about the shoulders—sunburnt complexion—hair black, but beginning to turn grey—features regular—eyes large and piercing—clean-shaved—dressed like a gentleman in a blue serge suit, probably cut by a London tailor—no special marks." That, he decided, was a fair description of the impression made upon him: it was not much to go upon. He returned to the office and wrote a short report of what had happened at the meeting, knowing that the incident would be reported in the morning papers and that he would acquire merit if he left his report on Superintendent Foster's table overnight. He was not proud of his performance at the meeting. It was sure to be said that he ought at all hazards to have followed the mysterious man home and have ascertained his address. He concluded his report by asking covering authority for calling upon Mr. Ralph Lewis in the morning and asking him whether he had ever been threatened or blackmailed.

The night was so fine that Patricia Carey proposed that instead of wasting time by searching for a taxi in Kensington, they should return home on foot.

"Well," she said, "tell me frankly what you thought of the speech."

"I was sorry he broke down," replied Dick Meredith. "It was the heat or the excitement, I suppose."

"Yes, poor man, but you heard enough of his speech to be able to give me your frank opinion of him."

"I did. Certainly he has the gift of the gab, like so many of his Welsh fellow-countrymen."

Patricia made a gesture of impatience. "Really, you men seem to be all alike. You don't seem able to recognize real genius in a person of your own sex. I suppose that you'll be saying next that he has no future before him as a leader in this country."

"Not at all. According to the immutable law of modern democracy, it is always the talkers who get to the top." Then, seeing that his remark had wounded her, he hastened to add, "I admit his eloquence and his extraordinary grip of his audience, but tell me frankly whether there was anything more. I was listening for some concrete suggestion of policy to get us out of our difficulties, and there was none. He wrung our hearts over his picture of the unemployed, but he gave no hint about what should be done for them."

"He did. You couldn't have been listening."

"That we should all give them our sympathy and love? Yes, but as he knows as well as we do, they want work more than sympathy, and he had no new plan to suggest because there isn't one that is economically sound, and there will always be unemployment until the world emerges from this crisis. No, like most of the rising politicians who want to make a profession of the business, he uses the unemployed as a step up the ladder. Tell me frankly—did you get anything practical out of his speech?"

"Perhaps not, but it was because we did not hear the end of it. It was a great shock to me when he was taken ill like that. When he stopped short and looked as if he was going to faint, did you see how he was staring at someone sitting two rows in front of us?"

"Was he? I confess that I didn't notice it. Did you see who it was?"

"No, because people began to stand up and blocked my view."

"Does Mr. Vance pay his political expenses—the rent of the Albert Hall, for instance?"

"Oh, dear, no. Mr. Lewis has quite large means of his own. His father was a big coal-owner in Glamorganshire, and he is now one of the directors of the company, so Mr. Vance told me."

"And Mr. Vance believes in him?"

"Entirely. Mind you, I can't say that I like all the men who come to Mr. Vance. One or two of them I distrust, but there is something about Mr. Lewis that quite disarms one. I suppose it is his modesty."

"His modesty?"

"Yes, for a young man just coming into fame he is extraordinarily modest; so much so that sometimes I've heard him speak quite pessimistically about his own future, which, of course, is absurd. Some day you must meet him. When you do, you'll be as enthusiastic about him as I am."

On the following morning Richardson made for the flat occupied by Ralph Lewis in Cromwell Road. He foresaw that there would be difficulties in the way when he asked for an interview, and there were. The lift carried him up to the third floor: a manservant answered his ring.

"I'm sorry, sir, but Mr. Lewis cannot receive any-body this morning. He has not been well."

Richardson took out his card on which was inscribed in printed capitals:

DETECTIVE-SERGEANT RICHARDSON,
C.I.D. NEW SCOTLAND YARD.

"Will you take this card to Mr. Lewis and tell him that it is important that he should see me for a few minutes?" Then sinking his voice to a confidential undertone, he added, "I think that Mr. Lewis would be sorry afterwards if he did not see me. I have some important information to give him."

The man departed with the card, shaking his head doubtfully, but in two minutes he returned.

"If you will kindly step this way, sir, Mr. Lewis will see you for a few minutes. He is in bed, but he will see you in his bedroom."

In his passage through the flat Richardson observed that it was very large and comfortably furnished in the most modern style. His feet sank into Persian carpets as he went. He noted that a luxurious bathroom adjoined the bedroom with a door of communication between them. His guide threw open the bedroom door and invited him to enter, closing the door behind him. The bedroom was large and luxuriously furnished. On the bed lay the man he had come to see, propped on pillows and clothed in a blue silk dressing-gown over his pyjamas. He seemed to have had time to comb his long hair: he was a picture of the interesting invalid—the poet prostrated by sickness. He was breathing rather quickly.

"Sit down, won't you, Mr. Richardson? I understand that you have something to tell me."

"Yes, sir, but before I begin, may I ask you whether you have ever been troubled by threats of violence, or by blackmailers?"

The effect of his words was such that Richardson wondered what the doctor would say if he came in at that moment. The man turned pale and made a brave attempt not to fall back on his pillows. He could not control his breathing, though he caught his breath in an attempt to keep it regular and natural. He tried to speak, but could only whisper hoarsely the word, "No."

"My reason for asking, sir, is that it has lately come to our knowledge that a man, or a gang of men, are plotting to cause you annoyance, and if you had told me that one of them had been giving you trouble, I should have ventured to give you some useful advice."

"Such as—?"

"Well, sir, people do not seem to realize the important change that has been made by the Courts in the hearing of such cases. Blackmailers have been encouraged by their victims' names being published in the newspapers. That is no longer to be feared. The police undertake the prosecution: the victim is described as Mr. X., and no one learns his identity, even if he is a well-known man. But in your case, as you tell me that you have not suffered in this way, such advice would be quite out of place."

"Yes," murmured the man on the bed.

"But I *can* tell you without indiscretion," continued Richardson, "that before your meeting last night at the Albert Hall we had received information that your meeting might be interrupted in a most unpleasant way. I was detailed to attend your meeting to protect you if necessary. I dare say that you noticed me on the platform."

Ralph Lewis tried to moisten his lips before trusting himself to speak. "I think I did," he faltered.

"Happily," continued Richardson, "I was not called upon to act, but I did notice something that gave me cause for suspicion, and I hope you will be able to help me. You see, sir, I have to make a report of what I noticed at the meeting."

"Yes?"

"And I want my report to be as complete as possible. Did you happen to notice a well-dressed man who was sitting in the third row below you?—a tallish, clean-shaved man with hair turning grey?" Lewis shook his head. "I thought I noticed that you were looking at him just before you had that attack of faintness, sir."

Again Lewis shook his head, but there was no doubt that the shot had gone home.

"Then I'm sorry to have troubled you, sir. I felt sure from what I noticed that you would have something to tell me. We are very anxious to get that man's name and address." He rose from his chair. "I have only to thank you, sir, for your courtesy in receiving me. Good morning. He turned at the door, instinct having told him that with a man as badly frightened as this there might be one last chance in appealing to his fears. I feel that I ought to warn you, sir, to be very careful when you go out to see that no one is loitering near the door of these flats, and also to caution your servant to be careful whom he admits to the flat.

Lewis's nerves had now reached the breaking-point. "Tell me, what is it that you fear?" he blurted out.

"If what has been reported to us is true, you may be in some personal danger, sir. If you care to see me confidentially at any time, I shall be at your service. You have my card. All you would have to do would be to ring up New Scotland Yard and ask for me personally."

Chapter Ten

IT WAS past eleven when Richardson made his first appearance at the office: he went straight to Super-intendent Foster's room.

"Well, young man," said his chief; "you don't seem to have made much out of that meeting last night. I've just been reading your report." He took up the report, and on reaching the last sentence, he broke into a laugh. "Covering authority for visiting Mr. Ralph Lewis? So that's where you've been all the morning. There's nothing like cheek. When I was your age I'd as soon have thought of doing a thing like that without first getting the permission of the officer in charge of the case as I'd have thought of telling him that he was messing things up."

"I was afraid you might not like my going off like that on my own, Mr. Foster, but I wanted to catch that young gentleman before he had had time to consult his friends. You see, sir, he had been badly frightened last night."

"And you thought that if you frightened him a little more he might cough things up. I don't say that you were wrong in theory, but did he?"

"No, sir, he didn't, but he helped us nevertheless. When I put it to him that when he broke down I had seen him staring at a man in the audience, and as good as asked him for the man's name and address, he went all to pieces. For a moment or two he seemed to have lost the power of speech, but when he recovered himself a little he stuck out that he had recognized nobody in the audience, and that he had never been either threatened or blackmailed."

"You mustn't build too much on the direction of a man's eyes when he has a fit, or is on the point of fainting. I've seen lots of cases when the eyes seem to be staring at a particular point, but in fact the sight has gone from them."

"Quite true, sir. I've seen a case like that myself, but this was quite different. The man didn't faint, or have a fit: even the doctor who attended him in the waiting-room told me that he had the symptoms of a man suffering from a fright, and if you had seen him in bed this morning, when I was questioning him, you would have said that he was badly frightened. No, sir, I am convinced that it was the sight of that man that made him break down at the meeting, and that his behaviour this morning was a clear confession that he was being blackmailed and that he did not want the police to know it."

"I wonder whether the man he saw could have been this Poker Moore that Mr. Meredith told us about. Look here, Richardson; you saw the man and can give a good description of him. Why not get hold of Mr. Meredith's friend, tell him what you saw, and take a statement from him?"

"Very good, sir. If you can spare me now, I'll do it at once."

A telephone call to Dick Meredith's flat elicited the information that he was out, but would probably be found at his chambers in Fountain Court, Temple. The Underground carried Richardson to within a hundred yards of Fountain Court in a few minutes. From the painted list of names at the door he found "Mr. Richard Meredith's" chambers without difficulty and tapped at the door. It was opened by a clerk, to whom Richardson explained his business. He heard voices in conversation within.

"Mr. Meredith is busy at the moment. I will ask him when he can see you," said the clerk, who left him standing on the landing.

The voices sank to an undertone; the clerk returned.

"He'll see you now. There's another gentleman with him." It was not a very promising preface to a confidential interview.

Dick Meredith received him cordially and begged him to sit down. "This gentleman is Mr. James Milsom, the friend who gave me the information I gave you at Scotland Yard. If you have called about that, I think that it might be useful if he were present."

Richardson bowed. "He is the very gentleman I wanted to see. Since I took your statement, sir, things have been moving a little. I attended that meeting at the Albert Hall last night. I think I saw you there, sir?

"Yes," laughed Dick, "and I saw you in one of the seats of the mighty. I tried to catch your eye."

"It was a curious thing—Mr. Lewis breaking down like that, sir."

"It was. My friend and I were talking it over just before you came. What did you make of it?"

"That is the very question I was about to ask you."

"I thought that the man had had a sudden fright He was staring at somebody sitting two rows in front of mine when he fell to pieces."

"Yes, sir, he was, and I tried to get hold of that man, but the crowd was so thick that I couldn't get near him. But I have a good description of him and I should know him anywhere. Do you think that it could have been the man you spoke of—the man you called Poker Moore?"

"The only way of putting that to the test is to describe him to my friend here. He knows him well."

Richardson took a slip of paper from his pocket and began to read: "About five feet eleven inches in height—slim in body—rather broad about the shoulders—sunburnt complexion—hair black, beginning to turn grey—features regular—eyes large and piercing—clean-shaved—dressed like a gentleman in a blue serge suit, probably cut by a London tailor—no special marks."

While he was reading, Richardson became conscious that Meredith's friend was bubbling with suppressed laughter, which could be restrained no longer when the reading was finished.

"I'm sorry," gasped Jim Milsom as he wiped his eyes, "but that picture of my friend, Poker, was too much for me, as it would be for you if you had ever seen the blighter. 'Tall and slim, regular features, large and piercing eyes.' Oh, good Lord! Why, Poker is as short and round as a beer-barrel. And then, 'dressed like a gentleman in a suit cut by a London tailor!' Poker, dressed like a gentleman! Why, it's good enough for *Punch*! You can't blame me for laughing."

"No, sir, I can't," laughed Richardson; "but do you know anyone else in this business whom the description would fit?"

"No, I'm afraid I don't. Why, a dozen men in every London club would fit that description."

"And you can't arrange for me to see your friend, Poker Moore, sir?"

"I wish I could. I want to see him myself, but the man has clean disappeared."

"Would it be of any use to advertise, do you think?"

"What? Do you mean this sort of thing? 'If Moore, formerly of Canada, commonly known as "Poker Moore," will communicate with his friends, all will be forgiven.' No, Poker, if I know him, would not be drawn by any advertisement. You know, sergeant, while you were reading that description I couldn't help thinking of what Poker Moore would have done if he'd been in the Albert Hall last night. It would have been one of two things: either he would have bored a hole in the skin of that political guy on the platform with a six-shooter—and I may tell you that Poker never misses and always shoots to kill—or he would have vaulted on to the platform, taken the blighter by his back hair and choked the life out of him."

"Then perhaps, sir, it was as well that the man was not identical with Poker Moore," said Richardson dryly. Then, turning to Dick Meredith, he said as he rose to leave, "I suppose that you will be going down to Somersetshire the day after to-morrow, sir?"

"Yes, the case is to be heard on Friday. I shall see the Chief Constable before the hearing, and I hope to persuade him to withdraw the charge about the stolen car."

When Richardson had departed, Dick turned to his friend with a twinkle in his eye. "I believe that this is your first experience of the Scotland Yard sleuth. What do you think of him as a specimen?"

"I must admit that I rather took to him. Are they all like that?"

"I don't know. He is the first I have come across. But he seems to be a live wire."

"He may be, but I can't get over the description that he wanted to pin to my old pal, Poker."

"Well, he'd never seen your friend and you have. I think he's a credit to the Force. He's not spectacular like some of the sleuths who are always running into print. These British detectives keep the press from butting in except in cases where it may be useful and the figures of arrests and convictions are all in favour of our C.I.D. I don't know how the figures work out in Canada. The point about our people is that they go on quietly working as a team, and don't let go until they've got their man."

"I'll believe in them when they find Poker Moore for me."

Quite unconscious of these criticisms, Richardson paused on the threshold and looked at his watch. If Lieutenant Eccles were lunching with his uncle in Hampstead it would be a good moment for catching him.

The door of No. 23 Laburnum Road was opened by an elderly person he had never seen before—no doubt the new servant who had been engaged to replace the murdered woman.

"Is Mr. Ronald Eccles at home?" asked Richardson.

"Yes, sir. What name shall I give?"

"Just say that I am the person who came to see him a day or two ago."

This rather mysterious message had its effect. She returned to show him into the drawing-room, and a minute later Ronald Eccles made his appearance.

"Hullo!" he exclaimed, "it's you. What's gone wrong now?"

"Nothing that I know of, sir. I've come to ask you to let me take your fingerprints."

"Good Lord! What for?"

"Well, sir, you remember that we got in a carpenter to take out the broken kitchen window in order to let us get a photograph of some fingerprints we had found on the sash-bar. Well, we want to narrow down the inquiry, and in case it might be suggested that the fingerprints were yours, which of course they couldn't be since you were down in Somersetshire that night, I should like to have your prints to compare with those on the sash-bar."

"Yes, that's all very well, but suppose that the man who left his fingerprints on that window happened to have the same markings as mine?"

"That is quite impossible, sir. Out of nearly two hundred thousand sets of prints in the registry, no two are the same, or even approximately the same."

"All right then, go ahead. I'd rather like to see how the trick's done. Does it make a mess?"

"Not at all, sir. I have everything with me." Richardson took from his pocket a square of glass, wrapped in paper, a small rubber roller, wrapped in American cloth, and a tube of printing-ink. Under the curious eyes of Ronald Eccles he squeezed out a little of the ink and reduced it to a thin film covering the glass. He took from his pocket a printed form of stout paper which he laid on the table beside the glass. "Now, sir, if you'll kindly turn up your cuffs and come over to this table. I want you to leave your hand entirely passive, with the wrist a little below the level of the table. The thumb first, please." Very deftly and quickly he rolled the right thumb on the glass slab and performed the same motion with it on the square of the paper marked "Right Thumb." He did the same with each finger in turn, until all ten had left their impression in the appropriate squares.

"Now, sir, I must trouble you once more." He poured a little benzine on a rag, and cleared the finger-tips of ink. "Now, will you put all four fingertips of the right hand on this slab quite lightly?" When the fingers were in position he pressed upon them lightly and transferred them to the paper, and did the same with the fingers of the left hand.

"Why have you got to take them twice over?"

"As a precaution against my having put any of the first impressions in the wrong square, sir. That's all. Let me wipe your fingers with the benzine: then they will be as clean as they were before."

"And now that you've done the trick, I suppose that a lot of bald-headed experts will pore over those prints and say that they've seen the prints of a good many blackguards in their time, but never such a criminal lot as mine."

Richardson smiled. "Fingerprints are no indication of character, sir. That fact has been thoroughly established."

Eccles picked up the form and studied it. "I can't see how anyone can swear to the identity of a man with nothing but these to go upon. I can't see anything peculiar about these. Can you?"

"No, sir. Your two thumbs are what we call 'whorls.' The fingers are ulnar and radial loops, which are far the commonest forms, but in classifying them the ten impressions taken together would be quite distinct from any other set."

"Do you mean that these prints of mine are going into the Rogues' Gallery at Scotland Yard?"

"Not at all, sir. When we have compared them with the prints on the sash-bar they will be torn up."

Richardson rose to take his leave and bundled his tools into his pocket.

"'Don't go yet, sergeant," said Eccles. "Let me get you a drink."

"No thank you, sir. I never touch liquor."

"'What an extraordinary man you must be! You do all this work on water?"

"Yes, sir," laughed Richardson. "It's merely a question of habit."

"Then have a cigarette. I want to ask you how you think my case is likely to go down in Somerset. Will they stick me into prison, do you think?"

"No, sir. You have a very good counsel to represent you. Probably you'll get off with a fine for the assault. I'm sure I hope so."

"So do I. If they hot me for what I did those old women at the Admiralty will look down their noses, and perhaps send me a printed form telling me that His Majesty has no further need of my services."

"I feel sure that it won't come to that, sir. And now I will leave you to your lunch, or they will be telephoning from the office to know what has become of me."

Before returning to the office Richardson stopped at an ABC shop to stay his hunger with a sandwich and a cup of coffee. Then, mounting to the third floor in Scotland Yard, he caught the official photographer putting on his coat before leaving for lunch.

"I'm sorry to keep you from your well-earned meal, Philpott, but I want a print of those fingerprints you took from the underside of a sash-bar in Hampstead."

"Haven't you got one in the file?"

"I suppose we have, but I want another. I'll let you have it back when I've done with it."

"I don't like parting with my office copy," grumbled the photographer, "but if you want it, I suppose you must have it." He returned to the studio, and after a two minutes' search, produced the prints.

"Good man!" said Richardson. "There's no need to make another set of prints. When I say that you shall have these back I mean it. You'll feel like a boy scout who's done his good action while you're eating your lunch."

Richardson ran downstairs with his photographs and crossed the carriage-way to Scotland House, where the Fingerprint Registry was installed on an upper floor. It chanced that the superintendent had lunched in the building and was just back to work. He greeted Richardson with a friendly smile.

"Hullo, young man! What new job have you brought us?"

Richardson spread the two sets of forms on the writing-table. "These two sets of prints have to do with a case of Mr. Foster's."

The superintendent brought his glass to bear upon the set of prints taken from the sash-bar. "It seems to me that I've seen this set before—and quite lately too. I have it. They are the prints found on a window-frame in the house where a murder was committed."

"Yes, sir, they are."

"Well, why do you bring them to me when I've already reported that they are not to be found in the registry."

"Only to ask that they might be compared with the other set, which are those of Lieutenant Eccles—a man who came under suspicion in an earlier stage of the case."

The superintendent took up the other set and laughed. "Who took these prints? If it was one of our people it is the first I have heard of it."

"No, sir. I took them."

"Good for you! They are very well taken. But surely you could see for yourself that the two sets are quite different. You needn't have come to us about them. Oh, you want to know whether Lieutenant Eccles' prints are in the registry? If there's no suspicion against him, it would be a waste of the men's time. Still, we are not very busy just now." He examined each print with his glass and scribbled a formula on his blotting-pad;

checked it over, entered it on the form and threw it across to Richardson, saying, "Here, take this to the registry and ask them whether they've got it."

In the registry was another of Richardson's class-mates who was still awaiting his turn for promotion to sergeant. They exchanged greetings and then got to business. In two minutes it was ascertained from a scrutiny of the files in the appropriate pigeon-hole that the prints were not in the collection.

Richardson now carried his prints across the road and sought out Superintendent Foster.

"Well, young man, you've taken your time," said his chief. "What have you been doing?"

"I showed my description of the man at the Albert Hall to Mr. Meredith's friend—the man who knows Poker Moore—and he laughed at any suggestion that the two were the same. Then I went on to Hampstead and took Mr. Eccles' fingerprints."

"Good God! Didn't he object?"

"He did at first, sir, but after I had talked to him he let me take them. I wanted to compare them with those prints on the sash-bar in case any question should arise afterwards. Then I got the Fingerprint Registry to compare them. They were quite different. As an additional precaution they classified Eccles' prints and made sure that they were not in the registry."

"You seem to be filling in your time, but you know, Richardson, we mustn't be running two hares at one and the same time. It's the murder that we must concentrate on, and we're not getting on. All this business about protecting Mr. Ralph Lewis against somebody who doesn't approve of him is none of our business."

"Quite true, sir, but I can't help thinking that the same men may be concerned in both cases."

"Because that marked newspaper was found by Eccles in that stolen car? I shouldn't build too much upon that. It may have been a pure coincidence. No, we seem to be up against a dead wall. I had to tell Mr. Morden so this morning, and he didn't like it, I can tell you."

"Have you the file on your table, sir? May I look at that newspaper again?"

"Here, dig it out for yourself."

Richardson ran rapidly through the file until he came upon the envelope containing the marked newspaper. He spread it out and examined each page. On reaching the fourth an exclamation broke from him.

"Look at this, sir. Something's been cut out of this page." He pointed to the right-hand corner where a square had been roughly torn out.

"We have the date of the paper. Send round to Fleet Street for another copy."

"I will, sir."

But in the passage it occurred to Richardson that the paper usually put its regular advertisements in the same position. He sent off a patrol to Fleet Street, but while he was gone he scoured the office for an issue of that day's date, and learned that it was one of the papers supplied to the Commissioner, whose room was on the first floor. He dared not disturb so august a personage, but he did the next best thing, which was to consult the Commissioner's messenger. From him he learned that the Commissioner was out at the moment, and that it would be quite safe to abstract the paper from his table for five minutes. This having been done, Richardson dashed down the stairs with it in triumph, for the advertisement at the bottom right-hand corner of page 4 contained the hours of the boat-trains from London to Paris.

He showed it to Foster who exclaimed, "If your man's slipped over to Paris it's going to be the devil. But how could he have got a passport? They don't give passports to burglars, and if he got over with another man's passport it will be the devil's own job to trace him."

"Wouldn't the Paris police help us, sir?"

"You don't know them, or you wouldn't ask such a silly question. They are active enough and civil enough when a foreigner is suspected of having committed a crime in France, but if it's a question of getting hold of a man wanted in this country they promise everything and do nothing."

Chapter Eleven

It was the morning of the Petty Sessions at Bridgwater. Dick Meredith and Ronald Eccles had travelled down from London together the night before, and immediately after breakfast Dick had sent up his card to the Chief Constable of the County—a retired army officer—who received him at once.

"I have come down," said Dick, "to represent Lieutenant Eccles at the preliminary hearing this morning."

"Ah yes, my people seem to have had rather a rough time with him. The black eye he gave one of them is turning yellow now, but it gives him a most sinister appearance."

"The assault seems to me to be far less grave than the other charge."

"You mean the charge of being in possession of a stolen car? Well, I've had some correspondence with my colleague at Portsmouth, and I may tell you at once that I propose to withdraw that charge altogether, but the assault—"

You propose to proceed with that?"

"I can't help myself. When a young naval officer allows himself the luxury of blacking a policeman's eye, he must pay for the entertainment. If I were to withdraw the charge, I should have unrest right through the Force. You can see that for yourself."

"I quite understand," said Dick, rising to go.

The Chief Constable walked with him to the head of the stairs.

"There's one hint I might give you, Mr. Meredith," he said. "Don't let your client speak if you can help it. Some of the magistrates are touchy folk, very much on their dignity, and if he puts their backs up they might commit him for trial."

Dick Meredith sought out Ronald Eccles when he got back to the hotel, and broke it to him that he must plead guilty to the assault; that he must be seen and not heard, even if the Bench asked him what he had to say in reply to the charge. "After all, the police are going to withdraw that charge about the car, and if you were to try to justify hitting a policeman in the face, you would put the magistrates' backs up, and they might send you for trial."

"That's all very well, but the blighter I hit assaulted me first. If I plead guilty and say nothing, the Personal Service people at the Admiralty will say that a bloke who goes about assaulting policemen isn't fit to be put in charge of men."

Meredith laughed. "If it comes to that, I shall have a word to say about the provocation you received, but take my word for it, it won't. I shall enter a plea of guilty for you, and you must promise to keep your mouth shut."

"All right then; I promise."

"Come on then; it's about time we started for the court-house."

When the two entered the building they found a Bench of six magistrates dealing with cases of drunk and disorderly, and of dangerous driving. They were quickly disposed of. Then "Ronald Eccles" was called, and his name was taken up by a court official outside. Eccles surrendered to his bail and was ushered into the dock.

"I appear for the defendant, Your Worships," said Meredith.

"Is this the case of stealing a motor-car?" asked the Chairman.

"It was, sir," said the Chief Constable, "but we do not propose to proceed with that charge. Further inquiries that have been made—"

The flutter on the Bench became audible. A naval officer charged with stealing a motor-car did not come their way every day. It was as if the keeper of the lion-house had callously wheeled his barrow of raw meat past the den, leaving nothing but its scent behind him. A magistrate leaned across to the Chairman and prompted him.

"Surely, Chief Constable, this man was arrested while in possession of a stolen car? We ought to hear the evidence."

"With all due submission, sir, it would greatly hamper the police in their efforts to discover the real thief, who had merely offered this prisoner a lift and whose identity was quite unknown to him. I do not propose to offer any evidence on that charge, but I will proceed with the second charge—that of assaulting the police."

"Very well," said the Chairman, after a moment's hesitation. "We will hear the second charge." The clerk read it over, concluding with the words, "Do you plead guilty or not guilty?"

"I am instructed to plead guilty to a common assault, Your Worships," said Meredith.

The detective with the parti-coloured eye was sworn. He said that while in the course of his duty he had had to take the accused out of a stolen car, using as little force as possible, he became "wiolent," and struck him a "wiolent" blow with his fist on the eye, which he exhibited to the Bench; that he had seldom encountered such a "wiolent" prisoner in the whole course of his service.

Dick Meredith cross-examined him about the provocation he had given to the accused. Later he cross-examined the other detective, who was called to corroborate the evidence of the first, and when his turn came to address the Bench, he suggested that the police had used unnecessary violence as a provocation, and dwelt upon the fact that this naval officer had been the victim of a car-thief, who had left him stranded in the road and had gone off.

"He has pleaded guilty," observed the Chairman when Meredith sat down. The heads went together on the Bench and, as one magistrate appeared to dissent from the proposal, whatever it was, the Bench filed out to their private room to consult.

Meredith went over to the dock for a whispered conversation with his client, who was in an aggressive mood. "I'd like to have five minutes with that aggressive beak when he was off the Bench," was his first remark.

"Hush!" whispered his counsel. "If a policeman overhears you, you'll be for it."

"What will they give me, do you think?"

"A stiffish fine and costs, I hope."

The door leading to the magistrates' room opened and the procession filed in again. Dick Meredith observed with satisfaction that the aggressive one had his chin in the air like a man beaten, but defiant. The Chairman addressed the prisoner, deploring that an officer in the service of His Majesty should have so far forgotten his obligations as to commit a serious assault upon another servant of the Crown who was doing no more than his duty. "The police must be protected," he said, "otherwise there would be an end to law and order in this country. You will pay a fine of ten pounds and costs, or go to prison for a month with hard labour."

"The fine will be paid at once," announced Meredith, going towards the clerk's table.

After paying the fine, he stopped at the table of the reporters, who were packing up their note-books, and pleaded with them not to make a feature of the case with leaded type, urging that Ronald Eccles was an ornament to the Navy, and that any exaggeration of the case might damage a distinguished career. Judging from a remark made by one of them he felt that he had not wasted his time. "I'd like to shake hands with him. I've often wanted to black the eye of that detective myself."

On reaching the hotel, he found Eccles consulting a time-table in the hall. "Looking up our train back to town?" he asked.

Eccles hesitated a moment before replying, "Well, no; I'm afraid you'll have to travel alone. An old shipmate of mine is in hospital at Portsmouth, and now that I'm down in the West I feel that I ought to go and see him, poor devil. Look here, I haven't thanked you for pulling me out of this mess, old man. I think that you managed that gang on the Bench splendidly. At one moment I saw myself picking oakum in an underground dungeon swarming with rats! I shall have to push off now if I'm to catch my train to Portsmouth."

On the journey back to London, Dick chanced upon a short paragraph in his evening paper about Mr. Vance's journey of inspection of foreign prisons and reformatories, and felt that Mr. Vance must have a very alert press agent in his pay. The paragraph went on to say that his many well-wishers in this country who had been active in helping prisoners after their discharge were attending a luncheon at an hotel in Holborn at which it was hoped to hear an address by that "distinguished speaker, Mr. Ralph Lewis," on the lack of progress of prison reform in Great Britain. Since the episode in the Albert Hall, Dick had resolved to attend every meeting at which Ralph Lewis was to speak. He cut out the paragraph with his pen-knife and stowed it in his pocket-book.

His first act on returning to Chelsea was to climb one storey higher and tap at Patricia's door. She opened it in person.

"Why, they told me that you were away!"

"I've just come back from defending a case in Somersetshire."

"I hope you got the poor man off. Had he done anything very dreadful?"

"That depends on what you would call dreadful. He had knocked down a policeman with his fist, but I haven't come to tell you about that. I've come to make a confession."

"Then you shall make it over a cup of tea, however dreadful it may be. Tea will give me strength to bear it."

"Thanks, though I'm not sure that it will give me strength to make it. It's about James."

"You mean that something has happened to the little brute?"

"No, but don't let me stop you getting that strength-giving tea, and then I'll make a clean breast of it."

Patricia hurried out to her tiny kitchen, and presently returned with a laden tray. While she was pouring out the tea, Dick asked when she expected Mr. Vance home from his travels.

"Oh, not for a week or two. I heard from him this morning. Why do you ask?

"Because I have been dishonest enough to plan a little deception on him in your interests—a plan to foist another parrot on him in place of James—a parrot who is now in training to say the word 'Absolutely' in a Canadian accent without stopping to take breath for hours at a stretch."

Patricia topped in the act of conveying her teacup to her lips and stared at him.

"You're not serious? Do you mean that there is no longer any hope of recovering James?"

"To be quite frank, I'm afraid that my hope gets weaker every day, and I wanted to have a second string to my bow in case Mr. Vance came back unexpectedly. I couldn't bear to think of you losing your job through my carelessness."

"It was a mad idea. Mr. Vance would have spotted the fraud in the first five minutes. No, when he comes I shall have to make a clean breast of the business and stand the racket."

"The man who is training James's understudy says that he would defy the bird's own mother to detect the change, but I'm not going to relax my efforts to find the little brute, so we'll talk of something else. I see that there is to be a sort of public luncheon to-morrow to discuss what is being done for discharged prisoners by Mr. Vance's supporters, and that Ralph Lewis is to speak at it. Do you think that you could get me a ticket?"

"To go and scoff at him?"

"Not at all. Your belief in Ralph Lewis is infectious. I want to go and hear him again."

"I could give you a ticket and take you in, of course, because I am more or less in charge of the arrangements, but you wouldn't hear Mr. Lewis. His doctor has ordered him to go abroad for a change, and he is leaving by the boat-train to-morrow morning to join Mr. Vance in Germany."

"Never mind. I should love to go if you will take me. Who is going to do the talking?"

"Mr. Gordon Pentland. He's to be chairman at the luncheon. He's not much of a speaker, they say, and he's a retiring sort of man—in fact, I had some difficulty in persuading him to preside—but he has been doing wonderful work for Mr. Vance in getting work for discharged convicts, and he ought to have some very interesting things to tell us."

"Gordon Pentland? Who is he?"

"I don't know much about him except that he's keen on his work and a great believer in Mr. Vance."

"And Mr. Vance finances his work?"

"Of course. I doubt whether he has the means for financing it himself. I have to look after his accounts: they mount up to a pretty stiff total, but Mr. Vance pays them with a sigh, and says in his defence that he has a wonderful influence over the convicts and keeps a number of them out of prison; that his office is entirely staffed by reformed convicts. After all, difficult work like that can't be done for nothing, can it?"

"I should like very much to go and hear him."

"Very well. If you'll call for me at half-past twelve to-morrow, we'll go together. I ought to warn you that Mr. Pentland has nothing to do with the official Prisoners' Aid Societies. He says that the convicts don't believe in them, so he works only with the men who have failed to get work from the Central Aid Society after they've succeeded in getting their prison gratuities from the agent. Don't forget. Half-past twelve. I'll have your ticket ready for you."

At a few minutes before one a taxi deposited Patricia and Dick at the door of the Holborn Hotel, where a crowd of people—mostly women—were exchanging greetings. Among the few men Dick recognized a face he knew: it was Detective-Sergeant Richardson, who was standing unobtrusively against the wall of the hallway, scrutinizing each new arrival. A tall, dark man rubbed shoulders with Dick as he paused for a moment to shake hands gravely with Patricia before he passed on towards the cloakroom.

"Who was your friend?" asked Dick.

"That was Mr. Pentland, who is going to preside at the luncheon. He asked me how Mr. Lewis was, and seemed sorry to hear that he had been obliged to go abroad. Now I think that it's time for us to be going into the dining-room."

"Then will you lead the way?"

It was not so easy to move on as it looked, for the whole assembly had begun to move in the same direction. While the traffic jam was at its worst, someone touched Dick on the shoulder. He turned to find his Scotland Yard acquaintance at his elbow.

"Excuse me, sir, but can you give me the name of the gentleman who shook hands with this lady as he passed in?"

"Gordon Pentland, I believe, is his name. He is going to preside at the luncheon. Why do you ask?"

"Because, sir, it is the same man that caused Mr. Lewis to break down in his speech at the Albert Hall the other night."

"Are you quite sure?"

"Quite, sir. I should know him anywhere. You can see for yourself how he fits the description I read to you."

Dick Meredith could not help being impressed by the obvious excitement of a man who had seemed so calm and business-like when he had seen him at Scotland Yard.

"Do you think that you could find out his address for me, sir? It would be a great help to me."

"I will try my best, sergeant. I know that he runs an office somewhere for helping discharged convicts."

There was no time to say more, for he saw Patricia waiting impatiently for him while she was being jostled by the crowd pressing forward to the luncheon-room like beasts at feeding-time.

"I thought you were never coming," pouted Patricia when he rejoined her. "Come along, or we shall never find our places."

Everyone has attended a public dinner or luncheon at some period of his life and knows how perfectly the waiting is done and how thoroughly uncomfortable it is. The noise of conversation was so loud that all Dick could do was to consume his food in silence and wait for the moment when the toast-master should call for silence for the chairman's speech. Dick had observed that Pentland had spoken scarce a word to his neighbours, and assumed that he was ruminating over the speech that was expected of him.

The moment came at last: the noise was hushed; Pentland was on his feet. He began his speech in a low voice, but his enunciation was so clear that he could be heard in the farthest corner of the great room. His first subject was the absence of the distinguished man who was to have spoken in his place, with a few feeling remarks about the cause of his absence and their hope that his health would quickly be restored. Then followed a description of his own work among the most unfortunate class of their fellow-countrymen, whose fall from good citizenship might generally be traced to bad housing and environment; sometimes to the spirit of adventure turned into the wrong channel. Then came what everyone was waiting for—the stories. There were half a dozen of them—some humorous, some touching, some tragic. Much play was made with the wives who tried to keep the home together while the husband was away, working in the bleak air of Dart-moor, not at work that was congenial, for no man was to be pitied for having to toil at congenial work, but at strenuous and often useless work that was thoroughly uncongenial. Most of them went through that terrible ordeal cheerfully, and emerged from the convict prison no worse than they went in: a few were brutalized by the discipline and the lack of sympathy on the part of the men set over them, who were often brutalized too. It was only when they came out into free life again that one could get into their hearts and win their confidence. And so on for a liberal twenty minutes. Many of his audience seemed to have heard all this before; many of them, no doubt, were thinking how differently their idol, Ralph Lewis, would have treated the subject. At all events, they were showing signs of inattention which the speaker was quick to see.

He switched off almost abruptly to the subject of Mr. Vance's tour of foreign prisons—"the modern John Howard, whose movements were being so eagerly followed by his friends at home, and by none more than the poor convicts who realized all he was doing for them."

He sat down after calling upon an extremely boring clergyman, who talked as if he had a plum in his mouth, and raised his voice almost to a shout in order to bear down the buzz of conversation that had begun at the farther tables.

Dick turned to Patricia. "Did you know all this about our chairman's work?"

"No. You see, his society is a one-man show and draws no Government grant, and so it publishes no annual report. Its expenses all come out of Mr. Vance's pocket. How did you like the speech?"

"It interested me so much that I'm rather tempted to call at Mr. Pentland's office one of these days—that is, if you'll give me his address."

"It's quite a humble little place—just an upper room in No. 58 Charing Cross Road, but if you are thinking of going there, you had better write to him in advance. I have heard that he does not welcome visitors in office hours."

Like all other functions that humanity attends, the luncheon came to an end at last, and the company was free to disperse to its several destinations. As they were leaving, Dick spied the tenacious Richardson waiting on the pavement outside. With some difficulty he secured a taxi for Patricia, paid the fare in advance and thanked her warmly for the ticket for which he divined Mr. Vance would ultimately have to pay. He crossed the road to Richardson, who was still watching the hotel entrance. "Here is the address of Mr. Pentland's office," he said, putting the menu card into Richardson's hand, and not stopping to hear his thanks. The last he saw of him was a figure still patiently waiting for Mr. Gordon Pentland's appearance. He decided that he would rather be a comparatively briefless barrister than a detective officer.

Chapter Twelve

EARLY IN THE same afternoon Richardson entered the superintendents' room at Scotland Yard to report progress to his chief. He noticed an expression of settled gloom on Foster's face as he looked up from the bulky file of the Hampstead murder.

"Well, young man, have you brought me anything fresh?"

"I think I have, sir. Here is the address of the man who caused Mr. Ralph Lewis to break down at that Albert Hall meeting the other night."

Foster glanced at the address without any show of interest and threw it aside. "You seem to be barking up the wrong tree, young man. We are out to solve the Hampstead murder, don't forget—not to protect a politician who has said plainly that he doesn't need protection."

If Richardson felt that his enthusiasm was damped, he did not show it.

His chief continued, "These sensational newspapers have begun to print nasty paragraphs about us, publishing a long list of unsolved murders and hinting that the Hampstead murder will have to be added to the list. The Commissioner has read them and must have spoken to Sir William Lorimer, who sent for me this morning to ask how we were getting on with the case. I told him the truth—that for the moment we seemed to be up against a dead wall; that we had eliminated practically all the possible suspects, and that unless some fresh evidence turned up we might have to confess ourselves beaten. He said, 'But what about those letters that were found in Eccles' pocket-book?' I told him that we had carried our inquiries about them as far as we could; that the man who repaid the money-lender was probably the murderer himself and that he must have done it in order to throw suspicion on Lieutenant Eccles; and that if the other letter, which he called 'the blackmailing letter,' had any bearing on the case at all, we could get no clue to the writer because the only man who knew who she was had refused to tell us and there were no means of coercing him. He asked me whether I would like to have additional help. I said 'no,' not at present; that you were doing very well, though you were a little prone to waste time over side issues of the case. There! I've laid all my cards on the table."

"So Sir William isn't pleased with us, sir?"

"No, and he'll be less pleased still if we throw in our hands— in fact, Richardson, you may take this case as the turning-point in your career. For me it doesn't matter so much. I'm getting on towards retirement. Now sit down in that chair and we'll go over the entire case from the beginning."

Foster gave a statement of the known facts which struck Richardson as masterly as far as it went, but it erred, as he thought, in brushing aside matters, such as the marked newspaper found in the stolen car, as irrelevant—as the "kind of coincidence that is always cropping up in cases like these"—in fact, a red herring drawn across the trail of the main issue.

"You know, sir, I can't feel quite as you do about that newspaper and the field it opens up. I have a kind of conviction that it is going to prove the key to the whole mystery. You will admit that though the murder was committed by one man, he had a gang to help him. The kidnapping of Lieutenant Eccles in order to prevent him from being in the house that night, and what was probably the kidnapping of the man they call Poker Moore, could only have been done with the help of a gang. I feel that if you would only consent to my going on with that side of the inquiry, the solution of the mystery would come all at once, and we should wonder that we had not thought of it before."

Foster shook his head. "We must stick to the facts we know about the murder. In going over the papers I have found one point that we overlooked in that blackmailing letter—that there had apparently been an address, but it had been cut off." He drew the letter from the file. "Now, if you take this glass you will see a pen-mark on the border—the tail of a 'g' or a 'y' perhaps—and you will also notice that the paper is shorter than notepaper of this size in proportion to its width. Also you will see that though the top edge is clean cut and not torn, the edge isn't quite straight. Probably the person who cut off the address used a pen-knife without a ruler to guide his hand."

"Yes, sir, you're quite right."

"What do you make of that?"

"Well—that the person who cut off the address, knowing that the letter would come into the hands of the police, had a strong reason for not wanting us to find the writer."

"Exactly. Go up to the top of the class. Now you've got to concentrate on finding that woman."

"I tried to do that, sir, when I was down in Portsmouth, but both the County and the Borough Chief Constables told me that it was hopeless unless they had further information."

"Never mind about them. There must be another way of finding out. Now that Eccles is clear of his prosecution, you may find him more inclined to talk."

"I would rather tackle his counsel, Mr. Meredith, first. He may know."

"Yes, but there you would be treading on delicate ground. He might think that you were trying to induce him to betray a secret between lawyer and client and send you away with a flea in your ear."

"I won't give him any excuse for thinking that, sir."

"Very well, do it your own way, and if you have to go down to Portsmouth again I'll get you authority."

Dick Meredith chanced to be alone in his chambers when Richardson called at Fountain Court. Though his heart had bounded at the thought that his visitor must be a solicitor's clerk with a brief, Dick concealed his disappointment and received him cordially. "Come in, sergeant. I'm very glad to see you."

"I must congratulate you, sir, on your success at Bridgwater. I read of it in the newspapers."

"Thank you very much, sergeant. Won't you sit down?" Dick felt sure that detective-sergeants had not time to go round scattering congratulations among their acquaintances, and that there must be more to come.

Richardson took the proffered chair. "I suppose, sir, Lieutenant Eccles fully understood what an escape he'd had.

Some of these country magistrates are very severe on cases of assault on their police committed by men of some social standing. He came back to town with you, sir?"

"No, he didn't. He had to go to Portsmouth to see an old shipmate who is in hospital there. Why, do you want to see him?"

"I do, sir, but I suppose he won't be long away."

"I should think not. He said that he wanted to take the opportunity, on being in the West, to visit his friend in the Royal Hospital. He may come back this evening or, at latest, to-morrow." Dick showed no curiosity about Richardson's object in again wanting to see Eccles, and he turned the conversation to a subject that interested him far more nearly. "Have you made any use of that address I gave you, sergeant?"

"Not yet, sir, but I have no doubt that my superintendent will do so. I was told that the gentleman in question spoke at the luncheon. Was it a good speech?"

"Oh, just the ordinary sort of bilge that one hears at such meetings. It seemed to go down with the audience all right."

Richardson laughed. "I can see that you don't enjoy charity meetings, sir."

"I'm not fond of them, especially when they are mixed with feeding. They are too much like missionary meetings for my taste. The speakers feel bound to pull the long bow in order to fill the collection-plate, though in justice I must admit that no plate was passed round."

Richardson rose. He had got what he wanted—the name of the Portsmouth hospital where Eccles' friend was lying ill—and he had no time to lose. He took leave, and Dick was left to wonder what had been the object of his visit and why he was so anxious to see Lieutenant Eccles again. He had not tried to pump him about the writer of the letter in the pocket-book.

Late that same evening Richardson found himself in Portsmouth again. He deposited his bag at a modest hostelry and strolled out to the Royal Hospital, where he ascertained from the doorkeeper that the secretary could be seen in his office at 10 a.m. On the way back to his hotel he looked in at the Borough Police Station and introduced himself to the night-duty inspector.

"I've looked in to ask whether you have got any farther with that car-stealing case, inspector."

"Which one? We have two or three cars stolen every week."

"I mean the car that was stolen by a man who posed as one of your detectives."

"Oh, that case! No, he's not been caught yet. I read to-day that the young fool of a naval officer who was found in possession of it got off with a ten-pound fine. What were the magistrates thinking of? Ten pounds! Why, they're asking for it."

"I suppose that your officer who's in charge of the case hasn't overlooked the possibility of that sham detective being an ex-convict?"

"I don't know, I'm sure. Why? Are you interested in the case?"

Richardson explained how the theft of the car was linked up with the Hampstead murder case on which he was engaged, but the inspector did not show much interest, having, no doubt, more to interest him nearer home. Richardson wished him good night and returned to his hotel.

The following morning was fine and sunny. Richardson set out to walk to the hospital. On the way he came upon a traffic block: cars coming from the direction of London were held up by an ancient car whose engine had conked out and was blocking the road. He stopped for a moment to see how it would be handled by the policeman who had come up, and was continuing on his way when his attention was called to a large and opulent-looking touring-car which slid noiselessly up to the block and stopped. It was driven by a chauffeur in livery, and in it was a single occupant—the man he knew as Gordon Pentland. At first he doubted the evidence of his eyes: one might easily be mistaken in a man with a motoring-cap pulled down over his face, but when the man stood up to get a better view of the obstruction, he had no doubt left—Gordon Pentland it was. From long habit as a London police officer, he noted the register number of the car, and jotted it down in his notebook. What was the man doing down in Portsmouth? That was a matter to be looked into.

He found the hospital secretary both competent and helpful when he had explained his business.

"I fancy," he said, "that we shall have difficulty with the house surgeon when I tell him that a detective from the Yard wants to question one of his patients. You know what doctors are. The house surgeon is omnipotent here when he digs his toes in. Besides, he may say that the man you want to see is seriously ill."

"I shall not have to see him at all if you can give me the information I want," said Richardson. "All I want is his address and what his wife's Christian name is, if you know it. I have to find out whether she was the writer of a letter that has come into our hands."

"You say that you don't know the man's name."

"I don't, but probably you keep a record of visits to patients. This man, an ex-naval officer, was visited yesterday by a Lieutenant Eccles."

The secretary took down a ponderous diary and searched the last two pages. "Here we are! Ronald Eccles—is that your man?—visited a patient named Henry Manton yesterday. The man cannot be seriously ill if he was allowed to see a visitor unrelated to him yesterday."

He took down another tome and searched the index. "Manton, Henry. Page 247." He turned over the pages. "Here we are! Henry Manton, admitted on the 6th. Address—Thornhill Farm, Millborough, Portsmouth." (Richardson made a quick note of the name and address.) "Wife's name—Gwendolen Manton, same address."

"That's all I want to know, sir, thank you. I'm very much obliged to you."

The morning was still young. Richardson found a taxi waiting at the corner for a fare: he stopped to ask the driver how far it was to Millborough, and whether he knew Thornhill Farm.

"Millborough's a matter of two miles out of the town. As for the name of the farm, these little poultry farms are as thick as gooseberries, but I can soon find it when we get to Millborough."

Taxi-hire was sure to be queried in his travelling expenses, for detectives are not allowed the luxury of travelling in taxis when trams, buses, or "Shanks's pony" are available. Having ascertained from the taxi-man that there were neither trams nor buses to this suburb of Portsmouth, Richardson drove a hard bargain with the driver and got in. The drive was not inspiring, bounded as it was by two neat rows of brick villas and cottages, but after the first mile and a half the landscape changed to a series of untidy allotments, each dignified with the title of "Farm," because the occupants were engaged in rearing poultry, and were making so poor a business of it that they had no money to spend on gardens or paint for their fences. The "farm-houses," such as they were, ranged from single-storey bungalows to shingled cabins of unpainted weather-boarding. In the village of Millborough it was some time before the taxi-man could find somebody who had ever heard of Thornhill Farm, but at last a passing postman put him in the right direction—"the first lane you come to on the left. Thornhill Farm is a couple of hundred yards down the lane on the right. You can't miss it."

Just as they were about to turn into the lane the taxi slowed down to allow a big touring-car to turn out of the narrow lane into the high road. Richardson's heart gave a jump, for the car was the same as that whose number he had taken in the traffic block an hour or two earlier, and Gordon Pentland was sitting in the tonneau! There was no tar-paving in the lane: Richardson could trace the wheel-marks of the big car, and when his taxi pulled up at the gate of Thornhill Farm, his first concern was to scrutinize the road surface. Yes, it was plain that the big car had gone no farther, for here were the marks of the complicated manoeuvre of turning in the narrow lane. So the man who called himself Gordon Pentland had been paying a call on Mrs. Manton, and had motored down all the way from London to do it.

The farm-house at Thornhill was on a more generous scale than the others. At some time in its sordid little history it must have been more than a poultry farm, for there was a cowshed and a shed for farm implements now falling into decay. The farmhouse, too, was a two-storey brick building. Richardson guessed that it had come into the market cheap and had been acquired by its present tenants at an absurdly low figure. But the hand of decay lay heavy on everything. The front door and window-frames looked as if they had remained unpainted for years; mortar had fallen out of the joints of the chimney-stack; the garden was overgrown with weeds; a few dejected hens were scratching about the front door. There was no bell, but having paid off his taxi, Richardson rapped on the door with his knuckles. It was opened by an attractive-looking woman, not quite in her first youth.

"Mrs. Manton?" asked Richardson, removing his hat.

The lady smiled assent, and asked him to come in. Through the tiny entrance-hall she conducted him into the living-room, which was furnished with dilapidated second-hand furniture, a few photographs and cheap framed prints hung upon faded wallpaper which had begun to peel from the plaster.

"I'm sorry to hear that Mr. Manton is in hospital," said Richardson. "I hope that it is nothing serious. He is a friend of Lieutenant Eccles, I believe."

For a moment the smile died out of the lady's face. "Do you know Mr. Eccles?" she asked.

"Only professionally, madam. I should explain that I am a detective-sergeant from New Scotland Yard. My name is Richardson. You may have heard that some days ago there was a burglary and murder at the house of Mr. Eccles' uncle, and that a large sum of money was stolen."

She shook her head. "I don't quite understand why you have come to me."

"That is easy to explain. As Mr. Eccles was the only person who was aware that a large sum of money was in the house, some suspicion attached to him at first, and it was important to prove that he could not have been in London. He would not say where he was on the morning before the burglary, but there is now reason to believe that he was in this house. If you could confirm that it would remove every breath of suspicion, and would at the same time be of considerable service to the police."

"Though perhaps you would not admit it, I suppose that Mr. Eccles told you all this," said the lady bitterly.

"No, madam, for some reason that we don't understand, he positively refused to tell us where he was."

"Just like him! Well, there's no secret about it. He came here on a matter of business in response to a letter I wrote him. He was here for about two hours. I can't give you the exact date, but that was the only time he has been here since his ship came in."

"You have known him for years, I suppose?"

"My husband has. You see, they were shipmates for the whole of one commission before my husband retired from the Navy, and they were great friends."

"And you have known him—how long?"

"Oh, ever since my marriage I saw him off and on." Her ease of manner had returned to her, and she was now all smiles.

Richardson determined to play up to her. "I hope that your husband is succeeding in making your farm pay in these hard times. You must be a great help to him."

"I doubt if he thinks so, poor man. No, the farm doesn't pay. I doubt if it ever did before we were fools enough to take it."

Richardson heaved a sigh. "I come from farming people in Scotland myself, and it is much the same with my people."

"Mr. Eccles was good enough to help us once, and I believe that if he had liked he could have helped us out of our difficulties again. I was never brought up to this kind of life and I loathe it, but what can we do with bankruptcy staring us in the face. I can see plainly that we shall have to leave this place. It's awful for a girl who was accustomed to pleasure and gaiety and pretty clothes to be imprisoned in a place like this. If it wasn't for a few generous friends, we should have left it before now."

Richardson allowed a look of sympathy and admiration to appear in his face. "It must be a sad change for you. I've no doubt that in the old days you must have had gaiety and amusement, and—may I say?—admirers."

The lady sighed and languished. "It makes me cry sometimes when I think of those old days, when really I had everything I wanted. I scarcely dare to look in the mirror now; my troubles have changed me so."

"I think you are worrying needlessly. At any rate, you've kept more than your share of good looks, madam," said Richardson with forced gallantry.

"I'd like you to see how I looked in those days. Sit here a moment while I run upstairs and look for a photograph. I shan't be a minute."

"I ought not to give you this trouble, but I confess that I should like to see whether it is like my conception of you." Richardson scarcely recognized himself in this unwonted role, but the temptation to get her out of the room was overmastering, for as he had passed through the hall he had noticed, hanging on the hat-rack, a man's felt hat of strange exotic shape, and he wanted to examine it. And so, when he heard the lady's footsteps safely overhead, he slipped into the hall and took down the hat. The maker's name had disappeared; he tried it on his own head and found that it was large enough to come down well over his ears. Had the absent husband as large a head as this?

A moment later the woman was by his side, displaying a faded photograph of an overdressed girl with an arch smile, as if the camera had said something that amused her. She was pretty in a rather vulgar style.

"There! That was taken when I was eighteen. What do you think of it?"

Richardson could in that moment have qualified for the comedy stage. He caught his breath with admiration, and dwelt for a moment on the portrait as if he could not bear to part with it. "Simply lovely!" was all he said as he gave it back to her. The ice was broken, but though he felt that he had established himself in the lady's good graces, he was too wise to press his advantage by questioning her.

Chapter Thirteen

RICHARDSON covered the two miles back to Portsmouth on foot. He wanted to think. The case on which he and Foster were engaged had now become complicated by the disinclination of his superiors to give him a free hand to investigate side issues of the case, and yet he was now more than ever convinced that it would be in these side issues that the Hampstead mystery would be solved.

He was in time to catch an afternoon train to London—a train that reached Waterloo too late for him to find his chief at the office. He decided to have his interview with Lieutenant Eccles that evening, and not to leave him until he had succeeded in breaking down his barrier of reserve on the subject of his relations with the lady who signed herself "Gwen." During the train journey he occupied himself in rehearsing his method of attack, knowing how important it would be not to put the young man on the defensive from the start. By the time he reached Waterloo and was on the way to Hampstead by the Tube, he had settled his plan.

Mr. Eccles was at home, the servant told him as she showed him into the library and invited him to sit down. "Aren't you the gentleman who called the other day from Scotland Yard? I thought I remembered your face."

Two minutes later Ronald Eccles made his appearance: he seemed to be in a jocular mood, which was all to the good.

"Well, sergeant, I suppose that you have come to congratulate me on being still a free man."

"Yes, sir, I was very glad when I read a short account of your case at Bridgwater in the paper. I hope that you were satisfied with the way in which Mr. Meredith handled your case?"

"Yes; I suppose he did it very well. He knew what I was up against, but I can tell you that I didn't like being made to promise to plead guilty and keep my mouth shut under every kind of provocation. If he'd given me my head, I should have told that row of dead-beats on the Bench things about their policemen that would have made them sit up and take notice. There was one blighter in particular whom I'd have liked to meet outside the court when the case was over. He would have gone home to his family a sadder and a wiser man when I'd done with him."

Richardson laughed. "Perhaps, sir, it was just as well that you couldn't wait about for him."

"As it happened I couldn't wait. I had a train to catch."

"The three-fifteen to Portsmouth? Yes, sir, it's a good train."

Eccles stared at him. "How did you know that?

"I was down at Portsmouth this morning, sir. You wanted to visit your old friend, Mr. Manton, in the Royal Hospital. You'll be glad to hear that he's getting better."

"Well, I'm damned. Is there anything that you sleuths from the Yard don't know?"

"Oh, quite a lot of things, sir; in fact, I wish we knew more, but when I was at Thornhill Farm seeing Mrs. Manton early this afternoon—"

"Hell!" interrupted Eccles. "What in God's name took you out to that benighted hole?"

"I was merely making inquiries in your interest, sir. You will remember that you declined to tell us where you had been on the morning you left the ship, and it was this that prevented some of my colleagues from entirely dismissing you from the case. Well, sir, the result of my inquiries has entirely cleared up that part of the mystery. We had Mrs. Manton's letter to you—the letter signed 'Gwen'—which we found in your pocket-book in this garden, but we hadn't her postal address because the man who dropped the pocket-book had taken the precaution to cut it off. So we had to find her as best we could."

Eccles' face darkened. "I suppose she told you a lot of lies?"

"I don't think so, sir. She said that you had been very kind to them both."

Eccles was breathing hard. "Wretched little fool! What idiots naval officers are for falling in love with the wrong kind of women! I'll bet that she ran upstairs to bring down a photograph of what she looked like at the age of eighteen."

"She did, sir."

"And then she made eyes at you?"

"I don't know about that, sir. She made herself very pleasant."

"She would. Well, as you seem to know the whole story—"

"I should like to hear it from you, sir."

"Manton was my shipmate in the *Ariel* for a whole commission. He was my greatest pal ever since Osborne days. He was a few months senior to me, and when they started axing officers after the Washington Conference, he came under the axe, poor chap. It was a desperate business for him with no money and a wife to keep. You remember, it was the time when everyone was mad about chicken-farming. Manton knew as much about chicken-breeding as I do about breeding elephants. All he knew was that chickens came out of eggs, so you bought eggs and there you were with your fortune made."

"How was he going to hatch them, sir?"

"With a beastly contrivance they call an incubator. He found that farm you went to, just outside Portsmouth, and was going to sell his chickens and eggs to ward-room messes in the Fleet, but everything went wrong; the eggs addled in the incubators; the chicks he did raise moulted and died on him, and I had to lend them money to carry on. I had to borrow the money to do it."

"Including that loan from the Portsmouth money-lender, sir—the loan which we told you had been repaid?"

"Yes."

"You see, sir, the money-lender's letter was in your pocket-book which was stolen from you."

"That blighter, whoever he was, must have had it in for me."

"Only to cover up his own tracks, I think, sir."

A light dawned in Eccles' face. "You think that the bogus detective man was working with him to keep me out of the way while he was committing the burglary. No, because there was the man he arrested. He couldn't have been in the swim too."

"I think he was, sir."

"Look here, sergeant, if there is anything I can do to help you chaps run that gang to ground, I'll do it."

"There is one thing, sir. You can tell me whether Mrs. Manton had any male admirers."

"Had she not! She made poor Jack Manton's life a hell. You see, people who admire her style would call her pretty; she dances well and has plenty to say for herself. Poor old Jack Manton has been in love with her all the time though she behaved like a cat to him. Come, as you know so much, you'd better have the whole story. She was always threatening to leave him, and one day he came to me in an awful state. She had left him that morning—gone off with another man. He implored me to get her to come back to him.

"Well, I went to the address he gave me and found her in a swank hotel, all dolled up, waiting for her new man to come and take her out for the evening. To me she seemed the nastiest piece of work that ever God made, but for Jack Manton's sake I had to go through with it. I talked to her straight for a good half-hour; told her that she was behaving like a cat to my pal and that she'd live to regret it when it was too late, and all that sort of bilge, and, by Jove, I got her crying in the end. She wouldn't tell me who her fancy man was, and I don't know it to this day, but my talk must have had more effect upon her than I thought it had, because next day Jack rang me up to say that she'd come back. Well, then something had to be done about keeping them together. Jack had hardly any money, but he had heard of that little farm going cheap, and I lent him a little money to pay for fitting it up. I had to borrow it. Since then she has looked upon me as the man who has blighted her life, and whenever she's broke more than usual, she tries to blackmail me for funds to carry on."

"Did she ever talk about taking in paying guests?"

"Not that I know of. Why, has she got one?"

"I'm not sure yet, sir. Perhaps you can tell me whether Mr. Manton has an abnormally large head."

"What extraordinary questions you ask! No, I should say that his head was rather smaller than mine."

"I wonder whether you would let me try on one of your hats, sir?"

Eccles looked at him curiously, thinking, no doubt, that overmuch sleuthing had affected his brain. Richardson had to repeat his request. Eccles went out into the hall and returned with a hat: it proved to be a little small for his visitor.

"Thank you, sir," said Richardson, returning the hat. "I ought to explain that there was a hat in the hall at Thornhill

Farm and that I took the liberty of trying it on while Mrs. Manton was upstairs. It came down over my ears. That is why I asked you whether she was taking in paying guests. And now I mustn't keep you any longer, sir. I shall keep what you have told me this evening quite confidential."

When Superintendent Foster reached his office next morning he found Richardson waiting for him in the passage with a written report in his hand. He had spent the previous evening in reducing his discoveries at Portsmouth to writing.

"Here's my report, sir."

"Here! Don't run away. Come in here and tell me what you found out down there." He led the way into the superintendents' room.

"Well, sir, for one thing, I have cleared up the question of how Lieutenant Eccles spent the morning before the murder, and I've seen the woman who signed herself 'Gwen' in that blackmailing letter. You'll find all the details in that report."

"Good! That's something done."

"But I've found out another thing that may prove to be more important. Mr. Gordon Pentland, the man who caused Mr. Lewis to break down in his speech at the Albert Hall the other night, drove down from London in his car yesterday morning and paid a visit to that woman."

"Did she tell you so?"

"No, sir; I saw him driving away from the house." He went on to tell Foster his reason for believing that a man was staying at Thornhill Farm during the absence of the husband.

"Ah," said Foster, "that fits in with what they told me at Pentland's office when I went to have an interview with him. The clerk said that he was away in the country for the day. Do you know, Richardson, that I'm beginning to think that you were right in what you said about the connection between the case of Ralph Lewis and the Hampstead murder. That is why I went round to that office in Charing Cross Road yesterday."

"I'm very glad you did, sir. What were the clerks like?"

"There were only two—both ex-convicts, I should say, by the look of them."

"You didn't let them know who you were?"

"Lord, no. I let them think that I was an employer of labour who wanted a handy man at low wages, and was interested in helping men who had been in trouble. Now, we've got to go carefully into this. Mr. Pentland, you say, is a friend of Mr. Vance, and runs an unofficial Aid Society for discharged convicts. You saw him yesterday paying a visit to a woman who is, on her own showing, very hard up, and you have reason for thinking that some man was staying in the house with her. There may be quite an innocent explanation. You know what these cranks are. They don't worry about the law. Suppose that Pentland is paying the woman to give house and home to one of his pets, who is wanted by the police for a crime, or for failing to report."

"Perhaps, sir," said Richardson doubtfully.

"I'm only putting the case to you. Like all young officers, you are prone to make up your mind and stick to it."

"Wouldn't the best plan be for you, sir, to see Pentland yourself and hear what he has to say?"

"No, that will have to be your job as you know all the details, but in the meantime we might ask the County Police to have discreet observation kept on that farm to ascertain whether any man is living there, and what he looks like."

Richardson looked doubtful.

"Well, what's wrong with the plan?"

"Only the lie of the ground, sir. Anyone loitering in that lonely lane would be spotted by the neighbours at once, and the word would go round that the farm was being watched by the police. The postman would spread it, and the woman herself would come out and ask the officer what he was doing there.

Besides, I doubt whether the Chief Constable has a man in the Force who could be trusted to keep discreet observation. The man would probably go straight to the house and ask for a list of its occupants. No, sir, I believe it would be better to see Mr. Pentland and be guided by what he says: then, if his answers are unsatisfactory, we might ask the County Constabulary to go boldly to the house and question the occupants."

"All right, well leave it at that. You'd better go and see Mr. Pentland this morning and turn him inside out."

Richardson's visit to the little office in Charing Cross Road was an experience which he always afterwards looked upon with satisfaction. He climbed a neglected staircase encumbered with waste-paper and cigarette-ends, to a door on the fourth floor and knocked. It was opened a few inches by a furtive little man of middle age, dressed in a dark suit of the cut which Richardson recognized as that of the prison tailor who made the liberty clothes for convicts a week or two before their discharge.

"Yes?" he asked in the tone of one who says, "What do *you* want?" at the same time closing the door an inch.

"I want to see Mr. Pentland," said Richardson blandly.

"Sorry, but he's out, sir."

"I don't think so. I can hear his voice. Let me in, please."

The man gave way, some subtle instinct having probably warned him with whom he had to deal. He slunk away into his den, and Richardson, entering the room, found himself in the presence of the man he had come to see and the girl he had seen at the luncheon with Dick Meredith.

"Must I go, Mr. Pentland?" she was saying as he came in. "Mr. Vance telegraphed to me from Stuttgart for that newspaper, so it is urgent. I'm sure it is somewhere in this file." She was going through a vast bundle of old newspapers.

"Don't go on my account, miss," said Richardson gallantly. "There is nothing private about my business with Mr. Pentland."

"Carry on, Miss Carey," said Pentland. His voice was cultivated and singularly musical. He turned to Richardson with a smile. "I didn't hear your name, sir."

"My name is Richardson. I have been instructed to call and ask you for some information about the work you are doing among ex-convicts."

"You represent a newspaper?"

"No, Mr. Pentland. It is an official inquiry from one of the public departments connected with the Home Office."

"I see. Possibly one of the official Aid Societies is becoming uneasy about the success of our work as compared with theirs. Well, we have nothing to hide. Many of the men who are discharged to the care of one of the official societies take their gratuities and disappear into space. They are not heard of again until they are arrested for a second crime. My friend, Mr. Vance, who is deeply interested in prisoners, when he became aware of this, decided to found an unofficial office to find honest work for these men, and knowing that I was equally interested, he invited me to join him and take charge of that side of his work. We enjoy no money grant from the State: all our funds are drawn from private sources. I may tell you confidentially that the greater part comes from Mr. Vance himself."

"I suppose that you keep a register of the men who come to you?"

"Oh, yes. The register is on that shelf if you care to look at it, and in this card-index is the history of each man as far as employment is concerned."

"Are you pretty successful in finding work for the men? It must be difficult with so many honest men on the dole."

"It is, and quite a number of the men have eventually to turn to the dole themselves. That is inevitable. If we continued to support them all we should go under. But we do find work for quite a large number. I make it a point never to hide the man's past record from the employer, and people are glad to give the poor fellow a sporting chance of turning over a new leaf. The important thing in keeping them straight is the personal touch: I make a point of seeing every man myself. I get many grateful letters from them afterwards."

"Do you employ any of them in this office?"

"Yes, I have two. They are very carefully chosen, and they have never given me a moment's anxiety. One of them must have opened the door to you."

"I suppose that sometimes you board some of them out in the country?"

Pentland stared at him. "I'm afraid that I don't understand what you mean. Board them out?"

"Yes, Mr. Pentland. I assumed that that was your object when you motored to Thornhill Farm, near Portsmouth, yesterday. I assumed that one of your protégés was boarded out there."

It was a bold shot and it told. Pentland reddened, but he did not lose his composure. On the contrary, he laughed quietly and said, "How funny that you should know Mrs. Manton too. I have known her for years—a nice woman. But I should not think of asking her to board out one of my black sheep. Has she anyone living in her house? She did not mention it to me when I saw her yesterday."

Richardson felt that the interview was not going as well as he hoped it would. The man was so entirely self-possessed, and everything he said was so entirely plausible. Dared he broach the subject of the Albert Hall meeting; say that he was on the platform and had divined the cause of the speaker's breakdown? No, a man so alert and self-possessed as this would affect to be amused by the implied suspicion; would speak feelingly about the extravagant calls a man like Ralph Lewis made upon his strength, and matters would remain exactly as they were.

During the brief silence Pentland turned easily to the young lady and asked how she was getting on.

"I've been right through this file, Mr. Pentland, and I can't find the paper Mr. Vance wants. I must go and telegraph to him."

"I wish I could help you, but I don't remember the paper at all."

"Oh, stop a moment. What's this?" She seized a slender bundle of papers and began to spread them out. "The paper I'm looking for may have got filed with these."

To Richardson's surprise the man's good manners fell from him like a garment. He sprang to his feet and almost snatched the bundle from her hands, exclaiming, "You came here to search the news-file, not to meddle with my private papers."

The action and the tone were so rude that Patricia could not fail to take offence. "I'm sorry," she said, gathering up her gloves and handbag. Bowing coldly, she left the room with her chin in the air.

Pentland stuffed the bundle of papers into a drawer in his writing-table and turned the key on it. Then turning with unconcern to Richardson, he asked "You were saying—?"

"I was wondering whether I had anything else to ask you, sir, but I cannot think of anything else. You do not publish an annual report of your work, I suppose?"

"No, because, as I told you, we draw no Government grant, and printing costs money."

"And you have no supervising committee?"

"No, my subscribers give me a free hand, and as long as they are satisfied—"

"Thank you, sir. Then that is all I need ask you." Richardson ran down the stairs with a faint hope of overtaking Patricia Carey, but he had given her a start, and to attempt to overtake a pedestrian in Charing Cross Road was a hopeless task. Yet he must see her, for she was his only means of knowing what was in the bundle of papers that he had seen locked into Pentland's drawer. His only hope was that Mr. Meredith, the barrister, might know her address. He went to Fountain Court.

Dick Meredith was on the point of leaving his chambers for lunch. Richardson met him on the landing, and explained as rapidly as possible the object of his visit.

"Not only can I give you Miss Carey's address, sergeant, but I will take you to her now if you like."

"But I don't want you to miss your lunch, sir."

"Oh, that's all right. I can lunch in Chelsea instead of the Temple. We'll take a taxi: it will be quicker."

Twenty minutes later Richardson found himself in Dick Meredith's flat, where he had been asked to wait while his host brought down Patricia from the floor above. The introductions were made and Patricia found herself talking to the man who had witnessed Mr. Pentland's "rudeness" to her.

"I've never known him behave like that before," she said. "His manners were always perfect, as they ought to be for a man who was educated at Winchester. Besides, what did I do? He had told me to hunt in that bundle of papers for what I wanted, and those papers were mixed up with it."

"Did you happen to see what the papers were?" asked Richardson.

"I had only time to read the top one before he pounced on it. It was a handbill, offering a reward for the arrest of a man named Owen Jones for murder. The reward, I remember, was five thousand dollars. There was a long description of the man, which I didn't read, and the information was to be given to the High Constable of Quebec."

"Owen Jones?" exclaimed Meredith. "Why, that was the name of the man that my Canadian friend, Milsom, spoke of— the man that his friend from the wild and woolly West was looking for to shoot."

Chapter Fourteen

RICHARDSON's report of his interview with Gordon Pentland was the subject of a conference in Charles Morden's room.

Morden viewed the matter from the legal angle.

"I can't see that we can find fault with a man who runs a private Aid Society for discharged convicts if he chooses to spend his own money on the business and draws no Government grant. He may even be doing some good, for in these days of an overcrowded labour market the official agencies can't be doing much for the men."

"Quite true, sir, but there are a lot of men gazetted for failing to report. How do we know that some of them are not being hidden away by this Mr. Pentland?"

"Suppose there are: suppose, for example, that the man with the funny hat which Sergeant Richardson saw hanging on the peg in that farm-house was an ex-convict, we should have to get evidence that Pentland was responsible for hiding him before we could deal with him. And after all, what has this to do with the Hampstead murder?"

"Not much so far, sir, I admit, but Sergeant Richardson thinks that it has."

Charles Morden smiled. "Now, Richardson, let me hear what case you can put up."

This summons took Richardson by surprise. At such conferences a junior is expected to take a back seat and let his seniors do the talking. He pulled himself together. "This is the way I see the case, sir. We know that the burglary and murder were committed by one member of a gang; that two other members were employed in kidnapping Lieutenant Eccles with the object of keeping him out of the way, we have good reason for believing that the man who posed as a detective was an ex-convict. In the car that he stole was found a newspaper with an announcement of the Albert Hall meeting marked in pencil. At that meeting I saw Mr. Pentland near the platform, and when Mr. Lewis broke down in his speech, I noticed that his eyes were fixed upon Mr. Pentland. We know that about the same time an American, or Canadian, called 'Poker Moore,' disappeared after letting it be known that he had come over to shoot Mr. Lewis whom he mistook for a man named Owen Jones. Then, this morning, while I was in his office, there was a curious incident. Mr. Vance's lady secretary, whom I know by sight as a friend of the barrister, Mr. Meredith, was in the office looking for some newspaper which Mr. Vance had telegraphed for. She couldn't find it, and when she took up another file of printed matter, Mr. Pentland snatched it from her hand very rudely. Up to that point his manners had been very polite. He said angrily that she was prying into his private papers. He locked the bundle into a drawer, and she took offence and marched out."

"But we don't know that there was anything compromising in the bundle."

"Pardon me, sir; I've just seen the lady and she tells me that the only paper she saw was a handbill offering a large reward for the arrest of a man named Owen Jones for murder. At this stage of the case I do not suggest that Mr. Pentland had any knowledge of the burglary or the murder, but I do suggest that the two cases concern the same men in some way and that we cannot solve the Hampstead murder without getting to the bottom of the other case."

"You think that the plot was hatched among Pentland's ex-convicts?"

"I do, sir. The men who go to the ordinary Aid Societies get their gratuities and disperse. When two or three of them combine in committing a crime it is because they live in the same neighbourhood and see one another every day. But Mr. Pentland's plan is to keep them together—he has two working in his office—and this crime was elaborately planned by a man of some brains and education. There are always a few of them in convict prisons—gentlemen who've gone wrong."

"And what do you think we should do now?" asked Morden with a twinkle.

"I think, sir, that the first thing to do is to get hold of the man that hat belonged to. On thinking it over, I believe that it was the same kind of hat that I've seen on the cowboy films."

"Why, it may be the man you call 'Poker' Moore—the man who's disappeared. Why shouldn't his friend go down there and see?"

"He could, sir, but if the man turns out to be an ex-convict, wanted for failing to report, Mr. Meredith's friend couldn't arrest him."

"Never mind that. We've got to get to the bottom of this business. What do you think, Mr. Foster?"

"I think that Sergeant Richardson had better get hold of Mr. Meredith's friend and get him to run down to that farm."

"Very well, do so," said Morden, turning to his next file of papers.

Richardson used the telephone to ask Dick Meredith for Milsom's address, and learned that at that hour he was always to be found at his club. To the club in Pall Mall he went; the porter sent in his name, and Jim Milsom tore himself from the bridge-table to see him in the hall. The club was one of those in which members were condemned to see their visitors in a sort of glass cupboard partitioned from the hall. He conducted Richardson into this uninviting den and asked him to sit down. "I've been reviewing my more recent past, sergeant, wondering which of my misdeeds have at last come to light. Have you brought the warrant with you?"

"It's not as bad as that, sir," laughed Richardson. "I've called to ask you whether you have had any news of your friend, Mr. Moore."

"Not a word."

"When you saw him last how was he dressed?"

"Poker Moore is no toff as regards clothes. I doubt if he ever buys a suit till he bursts out of the suit he's wearing through high feeding."

"He's a stout man, then?"

"No, not stout; just square—as broad and deep as he's long, like an old Dutch galleon."

"Has he a big head?"

"Just the biggest head you ever saw in your life—yes, and the biggest appetite."

"Then I think that I can give you his present address. Here it is."

"Lodging at a farm, is he? What's he doing that for? Did he tell you?"

"No, I didn't see him. I only saw his hat."

"A sort of cowboy's hat, bought at the beginning of the century. Why, that's 'Poker' all right. I'll go down to Portsmouth right away, but what shall I do with him when I've found him, I wonder. The man's out for blood."

"You might have a straight talk to him on the journey up—tell him the difference between London and Chicago in the matter of shooting people."

"I can see that you don't know Poker Moore if you think that talking would knock sense into him. When he's fixed his mind on a thing, there's no turning him by any amount of talking, and he's got his mind fixed on shooting a long-haired blighter of a politician. Anyway, I'll run down by an early train to-morrow morning and bring him back with me if I can."

Jim Milsom lunched early in a Portsmouth hotel, ordered a taxi, and drove out to Thornhill Farm at half-past one. Telling the taxi to wait in the lane, he rapped loudly at the door, and brought Mrs. Manton to it at a run. At the sight of a young, well-dressed Londoner she assumed a kittenish demeanour and asked what she could do for him.

"I'm told that you have a friend of mine staying here, madam—a gentleman named Moore. I should like to see him."

"You are just too late. Mr. Moore left me yesterday morning, and I was very sorry to lose him. He was a charming man."

"You found him charming? A brilliant talker? What did he do all day?"

"He sat in his room mostly—practising card-tricks, I think."

"Aha! That's my friend all right. Practising card-tricks? Did he ever show you some of his conjuring tricks? When he does them professionally it is apt to come expensive for the audience. Where has he gone?"

"To Germany, I understood. He had a telegram the morning he left, and he came downstairs with his bag and said, 'Goodbye, Mrs. Manton. I'm sorry I can't stay longer. I'm off.' 'You haven't any bad news, I hope?' I said. 'No, I've had good news. There's a man I want to see badly, and he's in Germany. What is there to pay for my board and lodging?' I told him, and he paid up like a gentleman. Perhaps you'd like to see his room."

Jim Milsom had no burning desire to see his room, but he reflected that there was always the possibility of picking up something left behind. "I should like to see it very much," he said.

The room she conducted him to almost shouted "Poker Moore" at him. It was a tiny room, barely furnished. The bed had not been made; cigarette-ends littered the floor; a dirty pack of cards had been dropped in confusion in the corner. Milsom looked about him with distaste, and his eye lighted upon a pink-coloured ball of paper—a crumpled telegram. He slipped it into his pocket, unnoticed by his hostess, who was profuse in her apologies for the state of the room.

"That girl is a lazy slut," she was saying. "Fancy her going off without tidying the room. I shall have to scold her properly. I suppose you wouldn't care to take the room for a few days.

I should do my best to make you comfortable. With my poor husband in hospital, and the farm and all to run, a paying guest would make all the difference."

"I wish I could," said Jim Milsom mendaciously, "but I've got to get back to town. I'm real sorry to have missed my friend. Good-bye!"

Safe from observation in the taxi he smoothed out the telegram and read:

"Address of man you seek Hotel Astoria Stuttgart Germany."

The message was unsigned, but the office of issue was Charing Cross.

So, someone who was in Poker's confidence had thought it worth while to telegraph the whereabouts of Ralph Lewis, knowing, of course, that this would at once remove Poker from the farm in the wilds of Portsmouth, where he spent his days practising card-tricks! But that was not the only mystery. What arguments could have been used to prevail upon Poker to immure himself in that ghastly little farm-house for a week or more? He could not have been frightened into it, for Poker was a man who did not know what fear was.

Finding no solution of these problems in the familiar English landscape racing past the window of his compartment, Jim Milsom decided that the man to see was the pleasant-spoken detective-sergeant who had broken up his bridge-party at the club on the previous day. His first act on getting back to his flat was to look up the telephone number of New Scotland Yard and ask for Detective-Sergeant Richardson. Some moments passed before that functionary could be found; the instrument clicked and he heard the competent and soothing voice he knew.

"Who's speaking?"

"James Milsom. Is that you, Sergeant Richardson? Look here, I'm just back from Portsmouth. I went down there on a fool's errand."

"You mean that the man who was there wasn't your friend, sir?"

"There was no one there. My friend left the place yesterday morning in response to a telegram."

"Indeed, sir?" There was a note of deep concern in the tone.

"I have the telegram here to show you. Hadn't you better come along to my flat right now?" He gave the address.

"I'll start right away, sir."

Ten minutes later the two men were seated in Milsom's luxuriously furnished sitting-room with the telegram before them. Richardson had declined any liquid refreshment, but had accepted one of Milsom's excellent cigarettes.

"You see where the telegram was sent from—Charing Cross?"

"Yes, sir, I do."

"I guess that you know who sent it, but you wouldn't tell me if I asked you. But why Stuttgart?"

"I understand that Mr. Vance, the gentleman who interests himself in prisons, is now in Stuttgart, and that Mr. Ralph Lewis intended to join him there."

"Oh, then the blighter who sent that wire must have known that. Look here, sergeant. Something must be done about this at once or we shall be having paragraphs in the papers headed, 'Shooting of an English M.P. by an American in Germany.' I suppose that if you were to go out to Stuttgart and put the German police wise about Poker Moore, you could get them to put him over the frontier."

"Perhaps, sir; but if I may suggest it, I think that it would be better if you went. This man, Moore, knows you and would be more inclined to listen to you than he would to a police officer. He might tell you how he came to be at Thornhill Farm and who sent that telegram. It would help us a great deal."

"Oh, well, I don't know that I mind going. I should have to cut one or two engagements, but nothing that really matters. I'll have to go round to Cooks' and find out about the ticket and the trains, and all that."

"I can do all that for you, sir, this evening, and ring you up. Would you be ready to start to-morrow morning?"

"To-night if you like."

"Very good, sir. I'll let you know the best evening and morning boat-trains in less than an hour. May I take this telegram away with me?"

"Yes. I don't want it."

"And if you are in time, and you find Moore at the hotel, will you send a telegram to Superintendent Foster at the Yard? Good night, sir."

Richardson found the tourist office in the process of putting on its curl-papers for the night, but on explaining to one of the seniors who he was and what he wanted, a clerk was kept back to attend to him. He used the firm's telephone to communicate the time-table to Jim Milsom. It was then too late to trace the sender of the telegram to Moore: that part of the inquiry had to stand over until the morning. He returned to the office to make his report to Foster and to write up his diary.

Superintendent Foster was not alone: a gentleman was sitting in a chair with its back to the door a gentleman whose back looked familiar.

"Oh, there you are, Richardson! I've been trying to get hold of you for the last half-hour."

"I'm sorry, sir. I had to leave the office on an urgent call."

"You can tell me about that presently. You know this gentleman—Mr. Meredith, who defended Lieutenant Eccles in that case in Somersetshire." The occupant of the chair turned round and greeted Richardson.

Foster continued, "Mr. Meredith has received information to the effect that Mr. Ralph Lewis is not in Stuttgart and has very kindly come down to tell us so, though I must confess that personally I don't know that the information concerns us at all."

"Yes, sir, it does. The man they call Poker Moore has just gone to Stuttgart to meet him there."

"The deuce he has!" exclaimed Meredith.

"Yes, sir, and your friend, Mr. Milsom, is starting this evening to try to bring him back."

"You take my breath away. I saw Mr. Milsom yesterday morning and he said nothing about it."

"It all happened rather suddenly, sir. May I ask how you know that Mr. Lewis is not in Stuttgart?"

"Mr. Vance's lady secretary—I think you know her—told me that she had had a telegram from Mr. Vance to that effect. It seems that letters addressed to Lewis had been sent to his care—I suppose on Mr. Lewis's own instructions—and Mr. Vance was put to the trouble of having them sent back. He telegraphed to her to stop it if she could."

"Does she know where he is, sir?"

"No; that is her difficulty. He seems to have told the servant at his flat that he was going straight out to Mr. Vance. He had his luggage labelled to Stuttgart. He must have changed his plans on the way."

"All the better, sir, as things have turned out. Mr. Milsom has promised to telegraph to my super-intendent when he gets out there."

"Well, Mr. Foster, I must be going. Let me know at once if I can be of any use to you."

When the two police officers were alone Foster stared at his subordinate in mock severity. "Well, young man, you seem to have been making the pace."

"I couldn't help it, sir. You were out of the office when Mr. Milsom telephoned to me to come to his flat. He was just back from Portsmouth. He had been down there, but his friend, Poker Moore, had already left for Stuttgart in response to a telegram, his landlady said. Fortunately he found the telegram in his room, crumpled up on the floor. This is it."

Foster looked first at the date and the office of issue before reading the text. "We'll have to get to the bottom of this. I suppose you didn't have time to trace the telegram in the Central Office?"

"No, sir; it was too late. I thought of doing it the first thing to-morrow morning.

"Yes, the sooner the better. And now, I've a bit of news for you. Our registry have had a reply from the Paris police. They say that if an officer will go over and point out the man we want they will send an officer with him to the place frequented by Englishmen of the criminal class, and they will take the usual steps for pushing him out of the country. I've never known them so obliging."

Chapter Fifteen

SUPERINTENDENT FOSTER's first concern was to secure Lieutenant Eccles as a travelling companion to Paris, for he alone was in a position to identify the man who had posed as a detective and carried him away in a stolen car. He called early at the house in Hampstead, and was relieved to hear that the gentleman had not yet gone out. "He has to rejoin his ship to-morrow, sir," whispered the maid as she showed him into the library.

This threatened to be a complication if it was true, but Foster knew ways of bringing gentle pressure to bear on the naval authorities in such cases.

"Hullo, superintendent, good morning," said Eccles, bursting into the room. "Come to say goodbye to me before my leave is up?"

"No, Mr. Eccles. I've called to ask you how you would like a trip to Paris at the public expense."

"To Paris? You're too late. My leave is up to-morrow."

"We might get it extended if you'd like to come to Paris."

"Now you're talking. What do you want me to do there?"

"Identify that bogus detective who carried you off in a stolen car."

"I'd cross the world at my own expense to do that, provided that I was left alone with him for five minutes."

"I can't promise you that satisfaction, I'm afraid, but wouldn't it be worth your while to know that he had been laid by the heels through your identification? In any case, you would have time to look round Paris a bit while I'm arranging things with the Paris police."

"Right! You may count me in. When do we go?"

"By the boat-train to-morrow if I can arrange for the extension of your leave in time."

Like most of his colleagues, Foster knew how to proceed with the Admiralty. Armed with a letter addressed to the Secretary by Sir William Lorimer, the head of his department, he called on the Director of Personal Services and explained that the matter was urgent in the interests of justice; that Lieutenant Eccles, who was due to rejoin his ship, the *Dauntless*, at Portsmouth on the following day, was wanted in Paris as a witness for the Crown to identify a prisoner who was to be arrested by the French police, and that no other witness was available. He asked for an extension of his leave for four days, and that he might be permitted to leave for Paris by the boat-train on the following morning. The Director kept the letter to be fed into the big machine, and gave covering authority.

Ronald Eccles proved to be a lively travelling companion. He had never been in France before, but he spoke a schoolboy French which fell somewhat short of Foster's. Everything he saw on the rather dreary journey to Rouen amused him, but he was eager to know exactly what they were to do on reaching Paris.

"We will take rooms at the Hotel Terminus, St. Lazare," said Foster. "Then, having deposited our luggage, I shall take you to the Prefecture de Police on the Quai where we will get hold of our man, and then we'll be guided by him. He knows the haunts of the man we are looking for. You'll see some of the seamy side of night-life in Paris."

"Where shall we dine? I'm getting hungry."

"At a little restaurant I know of in the Boulevard. I shall have to ask the French Commissaire to dine with us."

"That's all right, but I don't suppose that your little pub goes in for decent cooking. Why shouldn't we do ourselves well for once—at my expense, of course? Where can we go where they do you well?"

"There are hundreds of places to suit every pocket. I think that our best plan would be to let our Commissaire choose for us."

In the gloomy old building attached to the Palais de Justice, where Fouché founded the organization which became famous in serving many masters—Royal, Imperial and Republican—Foster presented his letter addressed to the Police Judiciaire to the *huissier* in dress-clothes, and they were shown into a waiting-room.

"They'll keep us waiting for half an hour, Mr. Eccles, if I know them," said Foster gloomily. "They seem to have no method of filing papers; the wonder is that they ever get anything done, but they do. Of course you've never seen a French law court. I'll speak to the *huissier*."

That official seemed quite indifferent to what they chose to do, and Foster led Ronald Eccles through a swing door into a lofty corridor where briefless barristers of both sexes were wandering up and down in conversation. Both sexes wore the black biretta and gown of the French Bar. The Englishmen peeped into one of the assize courts where a criminal case was in progress, and three judges were sitting in a row on a high dais, wearing much the same head-dress as the counsel who sat in rows below them. Ronny Eccles pronounced the effect as far gloomier than the British courts, where the wigs and the judges' robes imparted a touch of colour.

They returned to their waiting-room in the Police Judiciaire and found the *huissier* impatiently awaiting them.

"The second door on the left, messieurs. Ask for Commissaire Bigot." And he returned to his perusal of *Paris Soir*.

"Are these blighters always like this?" inquired Eccles, thinking of the contrast to the manners of officers from Scotland Yard.

"Generally. It depends on what public office you go to, but the French functionary is poorly paid, and he gives as little for his pay as he can."

Peter knocked at the door indicated and pushed it open. Three or four plain-clothes officers were sitting at a long, bare table, with files of papers stacked on the dirty floor beside their chairs.

"Commissaire Bigot?" inquired Foster.

A burly, good-natured-looking ruffian rose from his seat and came forward smiling. "Bigot, monsieur, at your service."

They shook hands.

"You are perhaps the Commissaire charged with the supervision of foreigners in Paris, monsieur?"

"Yes, monsieur. I have had the pleasure of seeing Monsieur before, but not this gentleman. Is he too a police officer from your famous Scotland Yard?"

"No, monsieur. He is a naval officer who has come over to identify the man we are seeking, in case we find him. We do not even know his name, or indeed that he is in Paris at all, but we have reason to think that he may be."

M. Bigot seemed a little surprised at this announcement, but he said, "Messieurs, this evening I shall take you to a certain bar which is the meeting-place of all the doubtful foreigners in Paris—particularly the English. It is an amusing place, but one in which it is wise to button up one's pockets."

"At what hour ought we to visit it?"

"At any hour after nine. We shall not visit it twice, for after they have seen me the bar empties itself."

"Good! Then there is time for us to dine together before our visit. My friend here desires to offer us his hospitality for dinner, and desires to taste the cooking for which Paris is so famous. What restaurant do you recommend?"

"There are restaurants and restaurants, monsieur. I do not recommend the most expensive. In them your money goes in paying for the uniforms of the staff, but I know one where the charges are moderate, but the chef is an artist. In days gone by he was chef to the Cardinal Rampolla, and cardinals are good judges of what is good for the stomach. Shall I take you there?"

Foster translated the proposal to Eccles, who voted for the cardinal's ex-artist. It being nearly seven o'clock, they took a taxi, which landed them on an ill-lighted *quai* scarce a stone's-throw from Notre Dame.

They were received by a man with pontifical manners, who led them to a table at the farthest corner of the little dining-room after relieving them of their hats and coats. He put a long menu before them.

"Look here," said Eccles, "this is quite beyond me. Tell Monsieur Bigot to do the ordering, and to do it well. All I draw a line at is snails."

Bigot did the ordering, and they sat down to wait over their *apéritifs* until the cook had had time to do himself justice. Foster did not waste his time. He was drawing out his confrere on the subject of foreign criminals and their habits.

"There are not so many here now as there used to be. The Russians and the Poles give us trouble, but not so much in central Paris as in the suburbs, but my specialty is the forgers, the blackmailers and the confidence men, and most of them are Italians, Americans or Englishmen. I think I know them all."

"What do you do with them?"

"When we catch them—and this is not so seldom as you would think—we take them to the Prefecture and use a little gentle persuasion to make them confess. If they are condemned, we expel them from France. After that there is generally a lull for a time. The others do not wish to be expelled."

"Do they prey upon the French?"

"Only rarely. Their victims are the other foreigners, but since there are fewer rich Americans now to prey upon they are less prosperous than they were."

"What about the drug smugglers?"

"Ah, there you have touched a point. Since the League of Nations concerned itself with them, we scarcely get a moment's peace. First it is the white slaves, then it is the stupefying drugs, and look you, monsieur, this is a land of liberty. If people commit crimes, yes: it is the duty of the police to arrest them, but if they sell stupefiers to people who wish to buy them, what concern is it of ours?"

Foster declined to be drawn into discussing the moral aspect of the drug traffic, but he asked whether any English were engaged in it in Paris.

"No, monsieur, no English. Italians, Roumanians, South Americans—all quiet men who give the police no trouble. They sell drugs to those who want them: so do the chemists. What of it? They do not cheat their customers."

All this in the interval of munching radishes from the *hors d'oeuvres*. And now arrived the first dish of a dinner that satisfied the appetite of even Ronny Eccles, and wine that might have come straight from the cardinal's cellar, and a glass of old brandy with the coffee. When they had finished, and Ronny had paid the bill and tipped the waiter, it was time to set forth.

A taxi deposited the party in the Boulevard des Italiens, and Bigot led them down a side street to the Bar des Anglais— the nocturnal rendezvous of all that was undesirable in the foreigners that haunted Paris. On M. Bigot's advice, the two

Englishmen stowed their pocket-books and watches in their most unlikely pockets.

The bar was crowded with men and women of all nationalities, but the men largely predominated. Most of the little tables were occupied, but a waiter, who appeared to know M. Bigot, made a swift raid upon empty chairs and dragged a table to the space nearest to the door. He took their order.

Scarcely had they taken their seats when a sudden hush fell upon the assembly whose conversation had been so noisy when they went in. It was evident that whispered word of the presence of a Commissaire had been passed round. Bigot was in no way disturbed by this testimony to his importance. He leaned back in his chair with a tolerant smile upon his lips, murmuring to Foster, "Advise your friend to keep his eyes open. Presently we shall see a number of these people leaving. They will have to pass our table. If he sees the man you are in search of, let him touch my arm as he is approaching. The English and the Americans will be the first to go."

With this admonition conveyed to him, Ronny Eccles kept his eyes open. The first to pass out were a number of men whom Foster recognized as frequenters of race-courses in England— bookmakers' touts and race-course thieves, who had doubtless come over for the races at Auteuil. Next, three Australians, with hats on the back of their heads, swaggered past. Bigot murmured that they were confidence men who preyed upon American tourists. Then a couple of furtive-looking Roumanian Jews.

During the pause that followed, the buzz of conversation rose: confidence was restored when it was seen that the unwelcome guest was not the forerunner of a police raid, but appeared to be acting only as a guide to "Paris by Night" for two more or less distinguished foreigners. Two men took that opportunity for leaving their table unobtrusively and making for the door, but as they neared the table the second man stopped, slapped his pockets as if he had forgotten something, and slipped back into the throng. It was too late: there had been mutual recognition. Ronny Eccles had spotted the man who had left him in the car, and the man had seen the only person who could identify him.

The manoeuvre had not been lost upon M. Bigot even before Ronny Eccles had reached over the table and touched him on the arm. Bigot's vast form was now in motion as if it were a bundle of springs. The crowd made way for him, leaving a clear lane to the fugitive's table. "*Viens, mon vieux,*" he said, as his powerful fingers closed on the man's arm. "You and I have something to talk about. *Viens!*"

"You're making a mistake, mossoo," said the man, but he went like a lamb nevertheless.

The incident was of such common occurrence in that establishment that it caused no confusion. There was silence for a moment as the procession passed, but that was all.

Ronny Eccles had hailed a taxi; Foster closed in behind the prisoner. There was no conversation in the vehicle as it drove to the Prefecture, for the prisoner maintained a stony silence. Only when they had climbed the stairs to the Commissaire's room, and were seated on either side of the oak table, did he open his lips.

Foster was the first to speak. "Your name is Richard Hathaway, isn't it?"

"It used to be. Now it is Ernest Brown."

"This gentleman has identified you as a man who posed as a police officer at Portsmouth on the 27th of last month. You will be charged with that offence in England."

"Will I? I'm not in England yet."

"Quite right, you are not, but the extradition proceedings won't take long."

"Oho!" laughed the man. "I thought you knew more about extradition law than that, Mr. Foster. To personate a police officer is a misdemeanour, not a felony, and there is no extradition for misdemeanours."

"You are perfectly correct, Brown, but stealing a car is a felony, and we shall apply for extradition on that. When we've got you over the Channel you will be charged with both offences."

This was a new factor to the prisoner, and he showed that he was disconcerted. "You'll have to prove it," he said sulkily.

"There will be no difficulty about proving both offences. You have already been convicted of similar offences. You know as well as I do that this is the wrong line to take. If you were to make a clean breast of it and tell me who put you up to this and paid for your journey to Paris, I should take care that the Court was made aware of it with a view to mitigation of sentence. Why not tell the whole story?"

As the man's lips remained obstinately closed, Foster went on, "We know that there was a gang of you all working together—the man you pretended to arrest was one of it—the man who broke into that house in Hampstead was another. You may find mitigation of sentence. Why not tell the whole murder if you keep your mouth shut."

"Murder? What do you mean?"

"I mean what I say. One of your gang broke into a house in Hampstead and murdered the maid, who was trying to protect her master's property."

"I know nothing about that, and you'll never be able to prove that I did."

"If you don't tell me all that you know, you'll be sorry afterwards."

"If I know nothing, there's nothing to tell."

"You can tell me who paid for your journey out to France."

"And if I told you that I paid for my ticket myself, you wouldn't believe me."

"All right, Brown. If you get a heavy sentence, don't blame me."

"What are you going to do with me now, Mr. Foster?"

"You'll stay in custody here until we get the extradition warrant."

"And how long will that take?"

Foster spoke in French to M. Bigot. "He wants to know how long the extradition proceedings will take, Monsieur, and where you will keep him in the meantime?"

Bigot flicked the ash from one of the English cigarettes which Ronny Eccles had given him. "Ten days, perhaps. As to where we shall keep him, you can tell him that we shall make him very comfortable." (This with an expressive wink.)

"Now then, you. Come along and I'll show you to your room in this hotel—bed, sanitation, bell to summon the *valet de chambre*—all complete." He rose and the prisoner did the same; he seemed to have an instinct that to be left alone with Eccles might not be healthy.

"It's a pity that Bigot could not give me just five minutes alone with that blighter before he took him away," said Eccles when the two were alone.

"For you it might be," said Foster dryly, "but I couldn't stand by and see murder done."

Five minutes later Bigot returned with a smile of self-satisfaction on his face. "He didn't seem to like his quarters, monsieur. He had so much to say that the gaoler had to go in to quiet him."

"Did he succeed?"

"Yes, monsieur. He's quite quiet now. Our gaoler has a way with him."

"Now for the formalities, M. Bigot."

"I've brought the forms with me, monsieur. If you will kindly sign your name here, I will complete the form. We shall hold the man on your authority until you send for him with the extradition warrant."

Foster signed the warrant and performed some additional rite which brought a flush of pleasure into the French officer's cheek.

"Good-bye, messieurs, and thank you very much. I hope that we may soon have the pleasure of meeting again."

"He seemed pleased," remarked Eccles as they were going down the staircase.

"So he ought to be. At the present rate of exchange it will be nearly thirty shillings to be charged to incidentals, but it was well worth that to get our man."

Chapter Sixteen

TWO DAYS LATER, Dick Meredith was reading in his flat after dinner when he heard the lift-gates clang back on his floor and the double rap of the hated Albert, the page-boy.

"What is it?" he asked impatiently. He hated to be disturbed in the evening.

"Two gentlemen to see you"—and in a lower tone—"one of them's the queerest-looking bloke you've ever set eyes on off the pictures."

"Did they give their names?"

"One did—you know him—Mr. Milsom—he's been here before."

"Show them up."

The lift clanked down and presently ascended. Dick opened the door to the visitors. Jim Milsom was followed into the room by a figure that might well have disturbed the composure of the loathly Albert—a short, square figure, clad in a garb not often seen in London, with a cowboy hat which he forgot to remove from his head.

"This is my friend, Mr. Moore," said Milsom. "We are just back from Stuttgart after an awful crossing."

"Pleased to meet you," croaked Mr. Moore.

"You look as if you both needed a drink," said Dick hospitably, going to the sideboard. "Sit down, both of you, and say 'when.'"

Moore withheld the monosyllable until the golden fluid was well up the glass. Evidently he did not believe in drowning his liquor.

"Dick, old man, we've a tale to unfold. My friend, Mr. Moore, being no orator, has asked me to do the talking. Shall I go ahead?"

"Please do."

"Well, as you know, I went out to Stuttgart to bring my friend back. I found him kicking his heels in the Hotel Astoria, having sampled the guests and found that none of them in the least resembled the man he was in search of. I asked him what had taken him to that miserable little farm-house near Portsmouth, and he told me. I said that he must come with me to Scotland Yard and tell the story to the police. He wouldn't hear of it; said that the police were a lot of bums and he made a practice of keeping clear of them."

Dick turned to Moore. "If that's your opinion of them, I don't wonder that you keep clear of them, but I should like to ring up a friend of mine, who is very much interested in your case, and ask him to come round and hear the story."

Moore gulped down a mouthful of whisky and nodded assent.

Dick went to the telephone and rang up Victoria 1212. "Will you please communicate with Mr. Richardson of the C.I.D. and ask him to take a taxi and come at once to Mr. Meredith. It is most important...I know, but you must have means of getting at him. He knows my address." He turned to his guests. "My friend, Richardson, is out for the moment, but they will find him. What was Stuttgart like?"

"Beastly. Johnnies in uniform saluting one another at every street corner by pointing at the skies, standing in the hotel lounge, peering at everybody who went in or out; bullying the wretched shopkeepers by going through their books; a hell of a place."

"But the Germans seem to like it—the herd-instinct, I suppose."

They continued in desultory talk for twenty minutes, Mr. Moore opening his mouth only to imbibe from his tumbler. At last Dick heard the welcome clanking of the lift, and Sergeant Richardson knocked at the door.

"Come in, Mr. Richardson. Sit down. You know my friend, Mr. Milsom, I think, but you haven't yet met Mr. Moore."

"Good evening, gentlemen," said Richardson, casting a keen eye at the broad figure with his hat on his head and a glass in his hand.

"These gentlemen have just arrived from Stuttgart in Germany," went on Dick. "Mr. Milsom was about to tell me why it was that Mr. Moore put up at that farm near Portsmouth, and I thought that you ought not to miss the story. Go ahead, Jim."

"Well, as I told you, my friend, Moore, strongly objected to coming to the police. He told me that while he was at his hotel in London a man called to see him and told him that he would take him to a house where he was bound to see the man he was looking for, because the man was carrying on an affair with the woman who lived there, and went down there every two or three days. That's right, isn't it, Poker?"

The broad man nodded.

"The man said that he had been down at the docks that morning and had overheard part of his conversation with his friend outside a bird shop; that he knew the lady at the farm, and was sure that she would make him comfortable. Well, they went down to the farm together; the lady was very forthcoming, and Mr. Moore decided to stay with her. But the man he was waiting for never turned up, and he had just made up his mind to clear out when he got a telegram saying that the man was in Stuttgart."

"Did the lady say anything about her relations with the man Mr. Moore wanted to see?" asked Dick.

"Yes, every morning she assured him that he was certain to come that day—otherwise Mr. Moore would have left the farm long before he did."

Dick exchanged glances with Richardson and asked, "Did Mr. Moore tell you why he was so anxious to see this man?"

"I was coming to that. He says that a few years ago he became involved in a quarrel in a saloon in Quebec; that this man, who was introduced to him as 'Owen Jones' threw the cards in his face, accused him of cheating, upset the table and attacked him; that there was a rickety balcony overhanging the river in that saloon, and that Jones pushed him through the glass door on to this verandah; that the railing gave way with his weight and he fell twenty feet into the St. Lawrence River, and Jones made no attempt to rescue him; that if it hadn't been for some boatmen crossing the river, he would have been drowned. As it was, when they pulled him out, he found that all the money in his pocketbook had been pinched. He was taken to the hospital and was in for an attack of pneumonia. When he got better he scoured Quebec for the man who had nearly murdered him, but was told that he had sailed for England. As soon as he had money enough to pay for his passage he came over, as he says, 'to square the account.' But on the voyage over he began to realize that with nothing more to guide him than a name it wouldn't be easy to find the man who had tried to drown him. It was only when he landed that he saw the man's portrait on a handbill and learned that his real name wasn't 'Owen Jones,' but 'Ralph Lewis.'"

Richardson had not forgotten the first instinct of a detective officer—to add to his collection of personal descriptions. "Excuse me, Mr. Milsom. Can your friend describe the man who called on him at the hotel?"

"You hear, Poker? What did the man look like?"

Moore put down his glass and frowned: for the first time he found his tongue. "Wa'al, he was a thin, wriggling sorter guy like a rat. He'd got his eyes too near together and yaller teeth—an' he kep' whispering-like—the sorter guy that'd go through yer pockets if he caught yer with yer eyes shut."

Richardson, who was making notes on the back of an envelope, looked up. "Did he stutter a bit in his speech?"

"Yessir, he did."

"You know him, Mr. Richardson?" asked Dick Meredith.

"Yes, it's a good description of one of the men I saw at Mr. Pentland's office in Charing Cross Road the other day. Hullo! Who's this?"

They had all heard the clash of the lift-gates: there was a sharp rap at the door. Meredith went to it with the intention of heading off the visitor: he found Ronald Eccles facing him. He had not seen him since his journey to Paris with Superintendent Foster.

"I've looked in to say good-bye, Meredith, and to thank you for all you've done for me. I'm off to join my ship to-morrow morning. But you've got people with you? I won't butt in. All I want is to ask you to do me a service—to keep me posted about what happens to that blighter who led me that dance in the stolen car. I should like to know that he gets it in the neck."

"Come in. I think that you know everybody here, except one."

Ronny Eccles strolled in, nodded to Milsom and Richardson, and halted before Poker Moore.

"I believe we've met before," he said. "Now where was it? I know. It was in that waterside saloon in Quebec when I had shore leave from the *Mermaid*."

"I don't remember you," said Moore bluntly.

"No? Well, that doesn't surprise me. You were in the middle of a heated argument with the gentleman opposite; the table went over and you both crashed through the glass door. You remember that?"

"Did you see what happened afterwards?" asked Meredith, deeply interested.

"No, I cleared out. You see, it was a first-class rumpus, and I didn't want the police to come in and start taking names. I was a youngster then and my old man was a stickler for propriety. If he'd read my name in the papers as being mixed up in a gambling row, in a dive like that, he would have laughed at my defence that I was studying low life for my general knowledge paper and would have stopped my leave for six months. The ward-room called him 'Holy Joe'; he's an admiral now."

"Anyway, you were long enough there to remember my friend, Poker Moore?" observed Milsom.

"Yes, I'd never seen poker played before, and I was watching his play. The other chap was half seas over—an excitable young ass—and when this gentleman called his bluff and laid down four aces—well, the youngster threw the cards in his face, accused him of stacking the deal, and went for him. Besides, this gentleman has a face that one doesn't often see—"

"A caricature of a face, you mean. No offence, Poker."

"I wouldn't call it that," replied Eccles, looking musingly at Moore. "I'd call it an unusual face."

"Would you recognize the other man if you saw him?" asked Richardson.

"I doubt it. He was a youngster; he was half drunk, and it was getting on for five years ago."

"I should like to have a word with you alone, sir, before I go," murmured Richardson to Dick Meredith.

"All right! Sit tight until they go." Aloud he said, "Jim, I hope that you've made it clear to your friend that if he meets this man, Owen Jones, in the street or anywhere else, he must keep his hands off him."

"Yes, he knows that. I'm giving him a shake-down in my flat until this business is cleared up, and he won't go out without me. I think that we'd better push along now and get some sleep after our journey. What about you, Mr. Eccles. Can we give you a lift?"

But Ronny Eccles preferred the humble Tube to Hampstead, and took his leave. Dick saw the three of them to the lift, and returned to Richardson.

"Are you beginning to see daylight, sergeant?"

"I think I am, sir, but there is still some way to go before we can act. We *must* get into touch with Mr. Ralph Lewis."

"I wish I could help you, but when a man deliberately goes into hiding, what can one do? Stop; there is one hope. Don't move from this room until I come back. I shan't be more than five minutes."

He ran upstairs and tapped at Patricia's door. He had not much hope of rousing her at such an hour, for probably she was in bed. But at his third knock he heard the sound of slippered footsteps, and the voice he knew so well cried "Who is it?" through the closed door.

"Dick Meredith," he called through the keyhole. "I must see you for a moment. It is very important."

The door opened a few inches, and he had a glimpse of Patricia in a pink silk dressing-gown, with the sleep hardly out of her eyes.

"I would never have dared to come at such an hour, but I know you'll forgive me when I tell you the reason. There is a detective from Scotland Yard down in my rooms. He wants to know Ralph Lewis's address."

Patricia opened her eyes very wide. "Why? It must be a mistake."

"No, he's explained it to me. Lewis is wanted as a witness in a murder case and they must get his address at once. Do you know it?"

"I do happen to know it, but he gave it me in confidence and told me on no account to give it to anyone else. He sent it only that I might arrange for forwarding his letters. What ought I to do?"

"If the Scotland Yard people insist on having it, I don't see how you can well refuse."

"Why can't they wait till Wednesday when Mr. Vance comes back? I'd far rather that he took the responsibility of giving it."

"Mr. Vance coming back? What about his parrot?"

The girl shrugged her shoulders hopelessly. "It can't be helped. I shall have to make a clean breast of it and be given the order of the boot."

"Rather than that, why not try that other parrot? My friend tells me that it now says 'Absolutely' without a fault. At least you can let me bring it round for you to see."

"Oh, I don't know—"

It was the first sign of weakening, and Dick resolved then and there to take advantage of it. He felt strongly elated. "Now, if you'll give me that address I'll go down to that man from the Yard. I promise not to give it to him unless he satisfies me that it will be to Lewis's advantage that they should have it."

"Oh well, if you promise that—his address is Hotel de Normandie, Veules-les-Roses."

"I'm sorry to have kept you waiting, sergeant," said Dick, returning to his room. "I had some difficulty in obtaining the address. If you'll lend me your note-book, I'll write it down for you. There! Veules-les-Roses is a little seaside place, not very far from Dieppe. By the way, I could only get the address by promising that it would only be used in a way that would be to Mr. Lewis's advantage."

"So it will, sir. I have felt sure for a long time that he was being blackmailed on account of some indiscretion of his youth. Now I think I have the key to the puzzle, but I can get no further until I see Mr. Lewis face to face and get the whole story from him. I can think of nothing that would be of greater advantage to him than to be freed for ever from a blackmailer."

Nothing further could be done that night. Richardson had the invaluable gift of dismissing his cases from his mind when he went to bed and taking them up afresh in the morning. He went home and slept well. Superintendent Foster found him waiting for him in his room when he reached the office next morning, and listened to his account of what he had learned overnight without interrupting him. They discussed the case in all its bearings, and Foster agreed that Ralph Lewis must be induced to return to England immediately.

"The only question is, who shall go over to fetch him?"

"I thought that you would do that, sir."

"Did you? I'm expecting to get that extradition warrant for Brown this morning. I shall have to go and fetch him over, and a man can't be in two places at once."

"Couldn't some other officer from Central go over for him?"

"What, let the case go out of the family? No, young man, we've borne the burden and the heat: you and I will jolly well see it through. Besides, I shouldn't be at all surprised to find that, after spending a week with the rats in one of those horrible dungeons in the cellars of the Prefecture, Brown will be talkative on the journey home. I may get something useful out of him. By the way, you haven't told me whether you traced that telegram that took Poker Moore away to Germany."

"I did, sir, but I didn't expect to get much from that. The message was handed in by a boy: it was signed 'Henry Wilkins, 57 Albemarle Street.' There is no such number in the street."

"The usual trick with blackmailers when they send telegrams. Well, I'll see Mr. Morden, and get authority from him for your journey to Veules-les-Roses, or whatever the place is called. Meanwhile you'd better get on with your report of what you've told me."

Richardson had half finished his report when the messenger called him to the superintendents' room.

"Mr. Morden is quite worked up over our case. He took me in to see Sir William, who made me go over the whole of the evidence, and he's worked up too. The upshot is that you are to go over to France to-night and bring Ralph Lewis back with you. It didn't seem to occur to either of them that he might refuse to come with you. They seemed to think that when once he had you to deal with, he would agree to do anything you told him to. Put that in your pipe and smoke it, and don't let your head swell."

Chapter Seventeen

THE VILLAGE of Veules-les-Roses, which is largely made up of hotels for summer visitors, lies fifteen miles west of Dieppe. Richardson was relieved to find that a motor-bus was leaving for the coast road half an hour after the arrival of the boat, for he knew that a charge for taxi-hire would be sternly disallowed by the Receiver's accountant. Throughout the drive he was haunted by the fear that Lewis had moved on and that he would have had his journey for nothing. On arriving at Veules-les-Roses, he determined to walk to the Hotel de Normandie, carrying his suitcase. He stopped at a tobacconist's to buy a box of matches, and asked the way to the hotel. His pronunciation of the language, which, to say the least, was Britannic, seemed to thrill the woman, for English tourists were becoming increasingly rare in the village, owing to the disastrous fall in the exchange, and his fellow-countrymen had left a good reputation behind them. With elaborate directions from the good woman, whose English was almost as unintelligible as his French, he had little difficulty in finding the hotel—a primitive-looking hostelry which had not yet modernized itself to attract the foreign tourist. A stout lady was sitting behind the desk in the hall; a couple of French children were playing a noisy game of hide-and-seek among the cane chairs in the lounge.

Richardson asked for Mr. Lewis: the lady looked blank: he asked to see the list of guests, adding that he would point out the name he was inquiring for. The lady pushed over to him a sheaf of registration forms which ought to have been filed at the police station, but were not. He ran through them: all were French names, their occupation being given as "commis voyageur," which Richardson rightly interpreted as "commercial traveller." It struck him as a strange hiding-place for a wealthy Englishman to choose. And yet—

At last he came upon the form he was seeking: "Lewis; *Prénom*, Ralph; born in Wales; Age, thirty-five; Occupation, blank." He showed it to the lady at the desk.

"Ah, Monsieur Levees. If Monsieur had pronounced the name correctly, I should have known. Alas, you cannot see him, monsieur. I have special orders to admit no one to see him."

"He knows me, madame, and he will blame you if I leave without seeing him," said Richardson in his broken French. "Give me at least the number of his room."

The lady was obdurate, but fortunately he had seen the number 27 scrawled in pencil across the form.

"Very well, madame, kindly let me have a cup of coffee in this lounge. Perhaps he will pass through it on his way out."

It being a matter of principle with all French hotel proprietors never to turn away custom from their doors, the lady shouted for Anne Marie, and a slovenly waitress in felt slippers went off to the kitchen with the order. Richardson consumed his coffee at peace with the world. He had surmounted the first fence: the man was in the hotel and could not get out of it unseen. The immediate question was how long he would have to wait. Fortune favoured him. The children's game had degenerated into a noisy wrangle in the corridor behind the lounge; piercing screams from the younger members summoned the hand of authority to quell the riot: the mother left her seat at the desk to restore order. This was Richardson's heaven-sent opportunity. Leaving five francs on the table in payment for his coffee, he slipped out to the staircase and fled upstairs to the landing above, where he had little difficulty in locating No. 27. No member of the hotel staff had seen him.

He knocked gently at the door. A bolt was shot back and it was opened a few inches, revealing the haggard features of Ralph Lewis in pyjamas and slippers and unshaven. He tried to slam the door in Richardson's face, but police officers are trained by experience to counter this manoeuvre and he found a booted foot in the way. He fell back, panting, and Richardson found himself in the room with the door shut and bolted behind him. He noted that there was no telephone in the room and that he was between Lewis and the bell-push.

"I'm sorry to have to intrude upon you, Mr. Lewis, but I have come all the way from London to see you."

"I told the people downstairs that I could see nobody," stammered Lewis. "How did you get the number of my room?"

"It was not the fault of the hotel people that I did. They told me of your order and refused to give me the number of your room. Never mind how I got it. I couldn't have my journey from London for nothing. Besides, I am here in your own interests —to protect you against serious trouble. You will remember that when I last saw you in London you assured me that you were not being blackmailed. We have since had abundant evidence that you are, and if you will give me a frank account of all that you have gone through, we can undertake to protect you."

"I haven't asked for any protection."

"No, I am quite aware of that, but without knowing it you have been in serious danger, and we were lucky in getting to know of it in time."

Ralph Lewis had turned very pale and his breath was coming short. "How do you mean in serious danger?" he stammered.

"I mean danger from a man who knew you in Canada as 'Owen Jones.' He had come over from Canada to shoot you, and if you had gone on to Stuttgart the other day as you intended, you wouldn't be alive to-day."

Ralph Lewis subsided on the bed and hid his face.

Richardson continued, "I know that you are suffering from nerves, like all the victims of black-mailers: otherwise you would not have thought of hiding yourself in a place like this."

"I came here for a rest. My health is not what it was."

"Yes, Mr. Lewis, I know that, and I also know more than you think about the cause of your breakdown. When you were travelling in Canada under the name of Owen Jones—"

"Who told you that?"

"A man who met you under that name in Quebec."

"Has that blackguard told you that?"

"The man I mean is a curious person, but I shouldn't call him a blackguard. You must remember that evening in the saloon in Quebec—that saloon with a balcony overhanging the river— when you played poker with a man, and accused him of cheating you, and had a fight with him."

"I see what it is. You needn't beat about the bush any longer. You've been sent out to arrest me for murder. I've been expecting this for months."

"No, Mr. Lewis. I haven't come out to arrest you for murder or anything else. I've come out to hear your version of what happened in that saloon in Canada, and induce you to come home with me."

"I don't believe it. I can't believe it. You *must* know what they accuse me of. You must have seen the handbills issued by the Quebec police."

"I have seen a handbill, but it wasn't issued by the Quebec police or any other police. It's a forgery."

"What do you mean?"

"You think that in a fight with a professional gambler named Moore, you pushed him into the river and drowned him. I had a talk with Moore the night before last. He is very much alive."

Lewis had been sitting on the bed with his face averted. He swung round now and faced Richard-son, his mouth open with astonishment. At last he found his tongue. "You can't mean the same man. The man I mean fell twenty feet into the river at its deepest part and went under. He couldn't swim. I think I must have fainted or something: otherwise I should have done something to save him. Anyone would, however low he might have sunk. They were all shouting. Someone pulled me back into the room. That's the last I remember until I found myself in bed in the hotel. I left Quebec next morning, and I've been haunted ever since by the sight of that water swirling in the dark and that awful splash as the man hit the water."

"Do you remember what the man was like?"

"However long I live I shall never forget him. He wasn't a man you could forget. He was a short, thick-set man with a broad face and dull eyes like a fish."

"Had he a big head?"

"Yes. I heard one of the men ask him just before we began to play whether he didn't have to get his hats specially made for him. Another thing I remember about him is that he never took his hat off. He was wearing it on the back of his head when we sat down to play."

"And they called him 'Poker Moore'?"

"Yes, or just 'Poker.'"

"Well, that was the man I was talking to in London the night before last. Look here, Mr. Lewis, as you've admitted so much, don't you think that you had better tell me the whole story from the beginning? What took you out to Canada?"

"My father had died the year before. As his only son, I came in for a good deal of money. He owned a lot of colliery shares, and it was the good time for coal-owners. I was what people would call a rich man in those days, but I'm a poor man now. Well, I thought of standing for the House of Commons and of making politics my career: I knew from my experience in the Oxford Union that I had some gift for stringing words together. I did not know that to succeed in public life one must have the thickest kind of skin, and that Nature hadn't given me. Well, at that time the shortest road to notoriety seemed to be a first-hand knowledge of the Dominions, and Canada was also a field for the investment of my spare cash. That was how I came to be in Canada."

"But why did you go there under an assumed name?"

"I went there under my own name, but I had a fatal itch for getting to know the seamy side of life as well as the other, and in my waterside rambles I used the name of Owen Jones whenever I put on the suit of clothes that I kept specially for these rambles. It was then that I first met the man who has ruined me, morally and financially. I met him in the hotel lounge. He was a public-school boy like myself, a few years older than I was, a charming companion and apparently a man of means. When he found that I wanted to study the seamy side of the city, he told me that he knew it inside out, and offered to act as my guide. He called himself 'Mr. Gordon' on these excursions; all the saloon-keepers and the loafers seemed to know him. When it came to drinking, I found that he had an extraordinarily strong head for carrying liquor, and, as I found out to my cost, I have a very weak one. Of course I had to be host on these occasions. I tried to be abstemious, but he wouldn't let me off. He said that 'glass for glass' must be the rule, otherwise the people would suspect me of being a reporter in search of scandal for a newspaper.

"One night he said he would show me a real gambling hell where I could study the professional gambler and his ways. Like a fool, I consented. He took me along narrow streets to the waterside, and into a horrid little saloon lighted with evil-smelling lamps. There he introduced me to this man, Moore, and whispered that he knew more about the game of poker than any man south of the St. Lawrence River. I had to stand drinks for the three of us, and after the third drink I felt that I was ready for anything—even to taking a lesson in poker from Moore himself. There was a crowd of people in the room—one, I noticed, was a youngster in British Naval uniform—and they all crowded round the table to watch Moore play. At first I had a run of luck and won money from Moore. He paid up without a murmur, but he said that he wouldn't play any more unless we changed the pack. I was elated at winning money from a player of his reputation, and, to say the truth, I had drunk more than was good for me. He called for a new pack from the bartender, and from that moment I began to lose rather heavily. It was extraordinary how those cards let me down. I remember one deal when I had a full hand—three aces and two jacks—and bet heavily on it, and when he called me, he put down four sevens. That sort of thing may happen once, or even twice, in an evening, but when it happens a third time even a man half stupid with bad liquor will guess that the cards have been manipulated against him. I stood it as long as I could, but when I detected Moore winking at a pal standing beside his chair, I lost my temper and saw red. I accused him of cheating. Most of the crowd took his side. I was past caring at that stage. I threw the pack in his face, shoved the table over and got him by the throat. The crowd stood back—I think that they expected him to start shooting, and they wanted to keep out of the way of stray bullets. Moore was less powerful than he looked. I shoved him towards the glass door: the door was rotten and gave way. Though I didn't know it, we were on a verandah built out over the river. Moore made a frantic effort to drive me back into the room. He couldn't shout because I still had him by the throat. I gave him a shove with all my strength and he fell back against the rail of the verandah, which cracked and gave way under his weight and he went over, very nearly carrying me with him. It seemed an age before I heard his body splash into the water. I believe that I sat down on the floor and cried like a child. Someone—it must have been 'Gordon'—pulled me back into the saloon. That is all I remember."

Richardson saw that his eyes were dilated with horror at the memory of that moment. He tried to bring him back to less dramatic events. "I suppose that you did not stay in Canada?"

"No. My friend, 'Gordon,' did everything—bought my ticket for the next steamer, sat with me in my room in the hotel, kept everybody away from me. He told me that there was a hue and cry for me, but that he would smuggle me on board the steamer without anyone knowing. When I got home I tried hard to forget about the business, and I allowed myself to be drawn into politics again through Mr. Vance, the philanthropist. It was nearly three years before I saw the man I had known as 'Gordon' again. It was at one of the periodical meetings of Mr. Vance's helpers. There was 'Gordon,' sitting right opposite me. Mr. Vance introduced him to the meeting as a man who had an extraordinary influence over criminals, and said that he had consented to take charge of a new enterprise—that of looking after those discharged convicts for whom the official Aid Societies could do nothing. After the meeting 'Gordon' came over to me and told me that now he was back in England he had resumed his real name of Pentland, and flattered me by saying that he had heard from Mr. Vance that I was the 'coming man.' He reassured me by saying that he thought that the hue and cry about Moore's death must have died down. I met him at meetings two or three times after that, and he did not refer to Canada, and then one day he came to me with a long face and showed me a police handbill, offering a big reward for the arrest of 'Owen Jones' for murder, and giving a very accurate description of me. He said that one of the men who had been in the saloon that night had brought it to him; that he said that he had recognized me coming out of a political meeting. 'It's all right,' he said; 'I've stopped his mouth by promising him five hundred pounds and his passage to the Argentine, but of course I can't afford to pay all that money myself. He seemed to be so genuine that I was fool enough to give him the money."

"You should have come to the police."

"I didn't dare to do that. Knowing, as I thought, that the man was dead, you would have been bound to arrest me. That was only the beginning. Every two or three months he used to come to me again with some fresh story about a man who had to be paid not to denounce me. I was on the high road to ruin. My colliery shares had almost ceased to pay, and in these days no one can afford to pay huge sums every three months or so. Pentland had devised a signal to warn me when I was in danger, in case he could not get to me in time. He put his right hand up to the side of his face and put his left hand up to his right elbow, like this. That meant that if I could not give him a private interview I was to send him money in notes. I had had some weeks of respite from his exactions when I had to speak at that meeting in the Albert Hall, and there was Pentland, sitting in one of the front rows. There was nothing in that. Mr. Vance's people made a point of coming to my meetings, but just when I was well under way in my speech I saw Pentland making that sign and I broke down. What made it worse was that I hadn't the ready cash to pay any more hush-money."

"Well now, Mr. Lewis, you can look the world in the face. Moore is very much alive. He was saved by some boatmen, who, by the way, seem to have robbed him of all the money he won from you. He has come over expressly to find you and get his own back, but you need not be afraid of that. I want you now to shave and dress, pack up your things, pay your bill and come over to London with me."

"To London?"

"Yes, to London. We want you to swear an information against Gordon Pentland of blackmailing you. There will be no publicity—first, because prosecutors in blackmailing cases need not give their names, and secondly, because in all probability Pentland will be charged with a far more serious crime and the blackmailing charge will be allowed to drop."

Ralph Lewis became a picture of irresolution. "I—I dare not go back to London and all this scandal."

"There will be no scandal at all. You went abroad for your health; you come back with your health restored. Lots of people in public life break down under the strain."

"But why should I swear this information?"

"Because without that we cannot arrest Pentland and so get the proof of a far more serious crime."

"Very well," sighed Lewis. "I'm in your hands."

Chapter Eighteen

THE KNOWLEDGE that the morrow was to be his decisive day and that he must get a good night's rest if he was to do justice to it, had its usual effect upon Richardson, and he slept like a log in spite of the acrobatic feats of the boat on a rough crossing. He reached New Scotland Yard in advance of Foster, and took his chief's approval for granted in making free use of the telephone by ringing up the police of all the Channel ports and at the Croydon aerodrome to warn them against allowing a gentleman named Gordon Pentland to leave the country. Scarcely had he sent the messages when Foster made his appearance. Richardson reported the steps he had taken.

"You seem pretty sure of yourself, young man. How do you know that we shall be in a position to make the arrest to-day?"

"Mr. Ralph Lewis has promised to be here at eleven o'clock to sign an information that he has been blackmailed by Pentland, sir, and on that you can proceed to arrest him, search his office for additional evidence and take his fingerprints."

"To see whether they tally with those thumbprints on the window-frame? And suppose they don't?"

"Well, sir, then we can proceed with the blackmailing charge, and when he's once under lock and key I shall be surprised if one of those ex-convicts of his doesn't come forward with something useful."

"Will you? I got nothing out of that rascal Brown on the journey over."

"No, sir? But I fancy that even Brown will be ready enough to talk when once he knows that his boss has been arrested."

"Had you much of a job to get Lewis to come over?"

"He dug in his toes at first, sir, but when I told him how much we knew already, he coughed up everything. Pentland has been bleeding him for months: if we can believe what he says he has nearly cleared him out. The man's nerve seems quite broken, but he cheered up when I told him that two days ago I had been talking to the man he thought he had murdered."

"Look here, young man, you'll be getting your head turned over this case. As you know, I didn't think much of your suggestion that Lewis's break-down at the Albert Hall and the kidnapping of Lieutenant Eccles and the rest of it had anything to do with the Hampstead murder, and now I see that you were right and I was wrong. I've told Mr. Morden quite frankly that the credit is due to you, and I shall say so in my official report."

"Thank you very much, sir."

"I quite believe now that Pentland planned the whole thing, but what I'm not sure of is his motive in stealing Eccles' pocket-book which led to the burglary and the murder. What do you think?"

"I think that Pentland's whole object was to get Eccles out of the way because he knew that he'd been present during the row, and he might know that Moore had been saved by those boatmen. He could get his movements from that woman, Mrs. Manton. Besides, he had seen in the papers that his ship had come in, and feared that somehow Lewis would get to hear through Eccles that Moore was still alive. So he went down to Portsmouth to take charge, followed Eccles into the hotel, and pinched his pocket-book to see if it gave any indications of where he was going. Then, finding the uncle's letter, he thought, 'Here's a chance.' More than two thousand pounds for nothing! And the chance of throwing the blame for the robbery on to the nephew. Whether he committed the crime himself or sent one of his gang of ex-convicts to do it we shall know when we get his fingerprints, but the measures taken for throwing the blame on to Eccles were certainly his—paying back the money-lender, and leaving Eccles' pocket-book on the scene of the crime. Though he is a fine, upstanding figure of a man, looking every inch a gentleman, I suspected him as soon as I saw what he did in that Albert Hall meeting, but I did not like to tell you so until there was better evidence to go upon."

The messenger looked in. "A gentleman to see Sergeant Richardson by appointment, sir."

"Show him in."

Ralph Lewis, looking weak and ill, but far more cheerful than when Richardson had parted from him, came into the room.

"This is Superintendent Foster, who is in charge of the case, Mr. Lewis."

Foster was at his best on such occasions. "Sit down, Mr. Lewis. You are going to do us a great service in helping us to arrest one of the worst scoundrels in London. I'm not going to worry you with making a written statement. You told all you have to tell to Sergeant Richardson yesterday. I have an information form all ready drawn up for your signature. All you have to do is to sign it if you find it correct. We will do the rest."

Lewis read the form with knitted brow and put out his hand for a pen. "Shall I have to appear in court?"

"If you do have to appear, it will be under the name of Mr. X, but probably you will not have to appear at all."

"It might be very disagreeable for me if I did. There are sure to be a number of people in court who know me by sight. The Press would be certain to find out my identity."

"But they dare not mention their discovery in print, and as for members of the general public, there is nothing disgraceful in being accused of a murder which was never committed. But, as I say, it is most unlikely that you will have to appear."

Lewis signed the document and asked, "When shall I know whether I shall be wanted in court?"

"This evening, or to-morrow morning. Sergeant Richardson will make a point of calling upon you. Good day."

"Now, young man, come along. We'll take Bow Street on our way and get a magistrate's warrant, and then hey! for Charing Cross Road!"

Getting the warrant took no more than five minutes, and five minutes later the two officers stopped at the foot of the stairs of No. 57 Charing Cross Road to consult for a moment.

"Suppose that he's not in," said Foster. "We mustn't alarm the men. I'll be an employer in search of a gardener, and you'll keep out of sight till you hear me whistle."

"Very good, sir, but I think he'll be here. I'm told that he's nearly always here in office hours."

They ran up the stairs to the second floor: Richardson hung back on the stairs while his duet knocked at the door. A moment later Richardson heard the whistle and raced to the door, which was being kept open by his chief. The ex-convict clerks had vanished into their back office.

Gordon Pentland received his visitors with cold politeness. "I don't understand the meaning of this intrusion, sir," he said, addressing Foster.

"Its meaning is that I have a warrant for the arrest of Gordon Pentland on a charge of extorting money with menaces, and I understand that you are the person cited in the warrant."

Even then Pentland did not flinch. "Gordon Pentland is my name. I suppose it is one of the stupid mistakes that Scotland Yard is always making. I suppose that I may see my solicitor?"

"Certainly, when certain formalities have been complied with. Before we take you to New Scotland Yard we intend to search this office. If you will hand over your keys, we shall do no damage to the office furniture."

Pentland took his bunch of keys from his pocket and threw it on the table. "Search what you like if you care to waste your time."

But the time was not wasted. Foster had had long professional practice in going through masses of documents and separating what was material from what was not. In half an hour he had a small pile of documents which he packed into a large envelope. Richardson, who had been guarding the prisoner, watched his proceedings and, pointing to a drawer in the writing-table, asked Pentland to move from his chair to give his chief more space.

That moved Pentland to break silence. "There is nothing but private papers in those drawers."

"I have to search them nevertheless," was the answer, as Foster fitted the key to the drawers. "Hullo! What's this?" He held up a packet of police handbills and examined them. "A handbill from the Canadian police with the imprimatur of a London printer! That's not bad."

"Oh, those!" retorted the prisoner. "They were printed for a play produced in private theatricals."

"You can tell that to the judge who tries you," retorted Foster, putting the bills into his envelope and opening another drawer. "Hullo, what's this?" He drew out a revolver and a box of cartridges.

"Was this for private theatricals too?" The prisoner making no reply, he asked, "Have you a licence for this pistol?"

"I don't remember. Probably not."

Foster stuffed the pistol and the cartridges into the envelope and gave the order to move off to the Yard.

The stairs being narrow, Richardson led the way, and Foster brought up the rear. As he was passing through the door a little rat-faced man, who had been hiding in one of the back rooms, touched him on the sleeve and whispered, "Excuse me, Mr. Foster. I dare say you remember me. You got me three years at the Central Criminal. I've served my sentence and I can give you some useful information about him." He jerked his thumb in the direction of the stairs. "I'm the chap that Brown pretended to arrest down in Portsmouth when he was playing the detective stunt on the naval officer. You know, sir, though the law doesn't allow you to pretend to be a police officer, it's no offence to pretend to be a prisoner. You can't touch me for that."

"I'm not so sure."

"Well, anyway, you won't—not when you've heard all I'm going to tell you. I'm King's evidence, that's what I am."

"You can come and ask for me at the Yard to-morrow morning at ten o'clock."

A passing taxi carried them down to Scotland Yard, where the prisoner was formally charged. He made no reply. A message had been telephoned to the Fingerprint Department and a sergeant was in readiness to take Pentland's prints. At first he objected, saying that he was an untried prisoner and that to take his prints was illegal, but Foster waved the objection aside. "If you refuse to have them taken quietly, we shall have no choice but to take them by force, and you will get no advantage out of that." He pointed to an apparatus with straps standing against the wall of the charge-room. "I'll make a note of your objection and you can raise the point before the judge at your trial."

Pentland shrugged his shoulders and submitted. Richardson followed the expert into the passage. "Have you got those thumb-prints with you—those thumb-prints found on the sash-bar of the kitchen in Hampstead?"

"Yes, here they are."

"Have a look and see if they tally."

The sergeant took a lens from his pocket and compared the prints in the strong light coming from the passage window. "Yes, the thumbs are identical. You can see them for yourself." There could be no doubt about them: the patterns in both sets of prints were perfect whorls. He slipped back into the charge-room, scribbled the information on a scrap of paper and pushed it over to Foster, who said, addressing the prisoner:

"It is only fair that I should tell you that a more serious charge is likely to be made against you to-morrow. You will appear before the magistrate to-morrow morning. In the meantime, if you wish to consult your solicitor, give me his address. You can see him this afternoon in Cannon Row."

Richardson was kept busy that afternoon. He was sent with the pistol and cartridges and the bullet found in the Hampstead house to the gunmaker who acted as expert witness for the police in shooting cases, and had to wait for his report, which was to the effect that the bullet which killed the dead woman could have been fired from the pistol submitted to him. With this Richardson returned to Foster, who said, "We are going to apply for a remand to-morrow, though of course we have now *prima facie* evidence sufficient for a charge of wilful murder, but I want first to hear what my rat-faced ex-convict friend has to tell me. It will be very useful on the adjourned hearing."

No one knows how the London Press gets hold of these things, but in the late edition of the evening papers there was an announcement in leaded type—"SENSATIONAL ARREST OF WELL-KNOWN PHILANTHROPIST ON A SERIOUS CHARGE." Jim Milsom brought the paper down to Dick Meredith and proceeded to take the entire credit of the arrest for himself. "Yes, sonny, if it hadn't been for me pottering about the docks we should never have known that Poker was still in the land of the living."

"If it comes to that, if I hadn't been called in by Miss Carey to deal with her parrot which was sitting on the fire, and hadn't let it escape out of the window, we should never have known of the existence of Ralph Lewis, and that intelligent young detective wouldn't have been on the platform at that Albert Hall meeting. And, by the way, what about that bird you told me you had in training? I ask because I hear that Mr. Vance is expected home."

"His education is getting on fine. Nine times out of ten he says 'Absolutely' in the accent of a Patent Medicine King: on the tenth he lapses rather badly still. I hope that Vance won't think that he learned the swear-words from the young lady."

"I'll come round for him to-morrow evening if you don't mind."

On the following morning Foster and Richardson were closeted with Bennett, the rat-faced ex-convict, for nearly two hours. He confirmed many of their theories, and told them much that would help them in building up their case against Gordon Pentland.

"Of course, sir, we all knew that he was a crook, the same as us poor devils, but he never took us into his confidence, if you know what I mean. All he ever did was to give us his instructions, and being dependent on him for our keep, what could we do but obey them? I'd sooner not appear as a witness against him in court, sir—not if you can do without me. You see, I'm a little chap, and Brown's a big one. If he gets off I should get it in the neck."

"Tell me," said Foster; "were you the man who was sent to take Moore down to that chicken-farm?"

"Yes, Mr. Foster, and I had to use a bit of tact to get him to go. The boss had told me what to say—that if he wanted to get the man he called Owen Jones, that was the place to catch him, because he came down there every two or three days, but he seemed to smell a rat and told me to get out. So I told him that I'd heard the police were after him, and if he didn't go down to the farm, the first thing he'd know would be that two 'tecs would come along to his hotel, take him off to Liverpool and put him on board a boat for the States. That got a move on him, I can tell you. I kept on telling him that it was the best place for catching Owen Jones alone, and, you see, Mrs. Manton told him the same thing, because she was the boss's mistress and he could make her say whatever he wanted her to."

But the little man had kept to the last a piece of evidence that to him seemed a fact of little importance. It was elicited by Foster.

"As a clerk in his office I suppose that you had a weekly wage? Did he ever give you anything extra?"

"Yes, sir—half a crown now and then if we went to him with a hard-luck story when he was in a good temper. You had to watch your step in choosing the moment. Once, I remember, he did us proud: it was just after Brown and me had got that naval officer put away. He called me in and shoved five pounds into me hand without me asking for anything."

"Five pounds in silver, do you mean?"

"No, sir—in Treasury notes."

"Have you spent them all?"

"I believe I've still got one left, sir." The little man emptied a pocket on the table, and from a pile of odds and ends—half-smoked cigarettes, matches, copper coins and string—drew out from this magpie hoard a crumpled Treasury note. Foster opened it out and scrutinized both sides of it. He took out his own note-case and tendered a new Treasury note in exchange, saying, "I'll buy this from you, Bennett. If you change your address you must be sure to let me know."

"Thank you, sir, I will," said the little man as he walked out.

"Anything special about that note, sir?" asked Richardson.

"This little bit of paper will hang Gordon Pentland, coming as it does on the top of those thumbprints and that revolver. Read what's written on the back of it."

Richardson read the words "E. Jackson" written in the untutored hand of the Redfordshire farmer.

"Yes, sir, that will hang him all right."

And it did.

At approximately the same hour Dick Meredith drew up at the door of his flat in a taxi, paid the driver and took out a birdcage containing a green Amazon parrot. He ran up the steps, hoping to avoid the hated Albert, but Albert was a youth who did not allow life to glide past him unobserved. He ran out from the porter's den.

"Bought another parrot for Miss Carey, sir?"

"No," replied Dick with hauteur and a contempt for the truth that should have made him blush, "it's the same one."

"Crikey!" exclaimed Albert, and turning, he made a dash for the stairs leading to the cellars.

With a sudden suspicion Dick dropped his cage and pursued him. The stairs brought him to the level of the backyard, the coal-cellars and boiler for the central heating, which were all in semi-darkness. He could hear Albert moving empty cases in the boiler-room. Suddenly from the gloom a sepulchral voice exclaimed, "Absolutely!"

It took but a moment to catch Albert by the collar and shake him, to grasp an improvised little cage made of kindling wood and wire and carry it into the light.

"This is Miss Carey's parrot. You stole him," said Dick.

"Absolutely," said the bird.

"I didn't steal him. I rescued him. He came down in the yard," said Albert.

"I'll deal with you later," said Dick, carrying the truant up to the hall and both cages up to Patricia's door.

Patricia Carey opened her eyes wide when she admitted him with his burdens. "Two parrots?" she exclaimed.

"Yes, James and his twin brother. You can now face Mr. Vance with a clear conscience. I'll keep his twin brother because I'm told that sometimes he lapses into language which Mr. Vance might not understand."

THE END